ISAAC ASIMOV'S
ROBOT CITY™

ISAAC ASIMOV'S

ROBOT CITY

™

BOOK 5: REFUGE
ROB CHILSON

A Byron Preiss Visual Publications, Inc. Book

ACE BOOKS, NEW YORK

This book is an Ace original edition, and has never been
previously published.

ISAAC ASIMOV'S ROBOT CITY
BOOK 5: REFUGE

An Ace Book/published by arrangement with
Byron Preiss Visual Publications, Inc.

PRINTING HISTORY
Ace edition/March 1988

ISBN: 0-441-37385-2

Ace Books are published by The Berkley Publishing Group,
200 Madison Avenue, New York, New York 10016.
The name "ACE" and the "A" logo are
trademarks belonging to Charter Communications, Inc.
PRINTED IN THE UNITED STATES OF AMERICA

10 9 8 7 6 5 4 3 2 1

CONTENTS

Through eighty percent of the history of *Homo sapiens*, all human beings were hunters and gatherers. Of necessity, they were wanderers, for to stay in one place would mean gathering all there was of vegetable food and driving away all there was of animal food—and starvation would follow.

The only habitations such wanderers (or "nomads") could have would have to be either parts of the environment, such as caves, or light and movable artifacts, such as tents.

Agriculture, however, came into being some ten thousand years ago and that introduced a great change.

Farms, unlike human beings and animals, are not mobile. The need to take care of farms and agricultural produce nailed the farmers to the ground. The more they grew dependent upon the harvest to maintain their swollen numbers (too great for most to survive if they had to return to hunting and gathering), the more hopelessly immobile they became. They could not run away, except for brief intervals, from wild animals, and they could not run away at all from nomadic raiders who wished to help themselves to the copious foodstores that they had not worked for.

It followed that farmers had to fight off their enemies; they had no choice. They had to band together and build their houses in a huddle, for in unity there was strength. Forethought or, failing that, bitter experience, caused them to build the huddle of houses on an elevation where there was a natural water supply, and to lay in foodstores and then build a wall about the whole. Thus were built the first cities.

Once farmers learned to protect themselves and their farms, and became reasonably secure, they found they could produce more food than they required for their own needs. Some of the city-dwellers, therefore, could do work of other types and exchange their products for some of the excess food produced by the farmers. The cities became the homes of artisans, merchants, administrators, priests, and so on. Human existence came to transcend the bare search for food, clothing, and shelter. In short, civilization became possible and the very word "civilization" is from the Latin for "city-dweller."

Each city was developed into a political unit, with some sort of ruler, or decision-maker, for this was required if defense of homes and farms was to be made efficient and successful. The necessity of being prepared for battle against nomads led to the development of soldiers and weapons which, during peaceful periods, could be used to police and control the city population itself. Thus, there developed the "city-state."

As population continued to grow, each city-state tried to extend the food-growing area under its control. Inevitably, neighboring city-states would collide and there would be disputes, which became armed wars.

The tendency would be for one city-state to grow at the expense of others, with the result that an "empire" would be established. Such large units tended to be more effective than smaller ones, for reasons that are easy to explain.

Consider that agriculture requires fresh water, and that the surest supply of that is to be found in a sizable river. For that reason, early farming communities were built along the shores of rivers such as the Nile, the Euphrates, the Indus, and the Hwang-Ho. (The rivers also served as easy avenues for commerce, transportation, and communication.)

Rivers, however, took work. Dikes had to be built along the shores to confine the river and prevent ruin through floods. Irrigation ditches had to be built to bring a controlled supply of water directly to the farms. To dike a river and to maintain a system of irrigation requires cooperation not only of individuals within a given city-state, but among the city-states themselves. If one city-state allowed its own system to deteriorate, the flood that might follow would disastrously affect all other city-states downstream. An empire that controls many city-states can, more effectively, enforce the necessary cooperation and maintain a general prosperity.

An empire, however, usually means the domination of many people by one conquering group, and resentment builds up, and struggles for "liberty" break out. Eventually, under weak rulers, an empire is therefore likely to break up.

World history seems to demonstrate an oscillation between empires (often prosperous, but despotic), and decentralized political units (often producing a high culture, but quarrelsome and militarily weak).

On the whole, though, the tendency has been in the direction not only of large units, but of larger and larger ones, as advancing technology made transportation and communication easier and more efficient, and as overall population increase heightened the perceived value of security and prosperity over liberty and squabbling.

As population grew, cities grew larger and more populous, too. Memphis—Thebes—Nineveh—Babylon—and then, eventually, Rome, which at its peak in the second century A.D. may have been the first city to have a population of one million.

The multi-million city became a feature of the modern world after the Industrial Revolution introduced enormous advances in transportation and communication. The nineteenth century saw cities of four million people and the early twentieth century saw cities of six and seven million people.

All through the last ten thousand years, in other words, the world has become more and more urbanized, and after World War II, the process became a runaway cancer. In the last forty years, the world population has doubled and the population of the developing countries, where the birth rate remained high, has considerably more than doubled. We now have cities, like Mexico City, São Paulo, Calcutta, with populations climbing toward the twenty million mark and threatening to go higher still. Such cities are becoming squalid expanses of shantytowns, endlessly polluted, without adequate sanitation, and with the very technological factors that encourage the growth beginning to break down.

Where do we go from here? Anywhere other than decay, breakdown and dissolution?

I tackled the problem of the future city in my novel *The Caves of Steel*, which first appeared as a three-part serial in *Galaxy Science Fiction* in 1953. I was influenced in my thinking by the fact that I happen to be a claustrophile. I feel comfortable in crowded and enclosed environments.

Thus, I enjoy living in the center of Manhattan. I move about its crowded canyons with ease and with no sensation of discomfort. I like to work in a room with the blinds pulled down, and at a desk that faces a blank wall, so that I increase my feeling of enclosure.

Naturally, then, I pictured my future New York as a kind of much more extreme version than the present New York. Some people marveled at my imagination.

"How could you think up such a nightmare existence as that in *The Caves of Steel*?"

To which I would reply in puzzled surprise, "What nightmare existence?"

I had added one novelty, to be sure. I had the entire huge city of the future built underground.

Perhaps that was what made it seem a nightmare existence, but there are advantages to underground life, if you stop to think of it.

First, weather would no longer be important, since it is primarily a phenomenon of the atmosphere. Rain, snow, and fog would not trouble the underground world. Even temperature variations are limited to the open surface and would not exist underground. Whether day or night, summer or winter, temperatures in the underground city would remain equable and nearly constant. In place of spending energy on heating and cooling, you would have to spend energy on ventilation, to be sure, but I think that this would involve a large net saving. Electrified transportation would be required to avoid the pollution of the internal-combustion engine, but then walking (considering the certainty of good weather) would become much more attractive and that, too, would not only save energy, but would promote better health.

The only adverse environmental conditions that would affect the underground world would be volcanoes, earthquakes, and meteoric impacts. However, we know where volcanoes exist and where earthquakes are common and might avoid those areas. And perhaps we will have a space patrol to destroy any meteoric objects likely to bring them uncomfortably close.

Second, local time would no longer be important. On the surface, the tyranny of day and night cannot be avoided, and when it is morning in one place, it is noon in another, evening in still another and midnight in yet another. The rhythm of human life is therefore out of phase. Underground, where artificial light will determine the day, we can if we wish make a uniform time the planet over. This would certainly simplify global cooperation and would eliminate jet lag. (If a global day and global night turn out to have serious deficiencies, any other system can be set up. The point is it will be *our* system and not one forced on us by the accident of Earth's rotation.)

Third, the ecological structure could be stabilized. Right now, with humanity on the planetary surface, we encumber the Earth. Our enormous numbers take up room, as do all the structures we build to house ourselves and our machines, to make possible our transportation and communication, to offer ourselves rest and recreation. All these things distort the wild, depriving many species of plants and animals of their natural habitat—and sometimes, involuntarily, favoring a few, such as rats and roaches.

If humanity and its structures are removed below ground —well below the level of the natural world of the burrowing animals—Man would still occupy the surface with his farms, his forestry, his observation towers, his air terminals and so on, but the extent of that occupation would be enormously decreased. Indeed, as one imagines the underground world becoming increasingly elaborate, one can visualize much of the food supply eventually deriving from soilless crops grown in artificially illuminated areas underground. The Earth's surface might be increasingly turned over to park and to wilderness, maintained at ecological stability.

Nor would we be depriving ourselves of nature. Indeed, it would be closer. It might seem that to withdraw underground is to withdraw from the natural world, but would that be so? Would the withdrawal be more complete than it is now, when so many people work in city buildings that are often windowless and artificially conditioned? Even where there are windows, what is the prospect one views (if one bothers to), but sun, sky, and buildings to the horizon—plus some limited greenery?

And to get away from the city now? To reach the real countryside? One must travel horizontally for miles and miles, first across city pavements and then across suburban sprawls. And the countryside we would be viewing would be steadily retreating and steadily undergoing damage.

In the underground world, we might have areas of greenery, too, even parks—and tropical growth in greenhouses. But we don't have to depend on these makeshift attempts, comforting though they may be to many. We need only go straight up, a mere couple of hundred yards above the level of "Main Street, Underground" and—there you are.

The surface you would visit would be nature—perhaps tamer than it might be, but relatively unspoiled. The surface would have to be protected from too frequent, or too intense, or too careless visiting, but however carefully restricted the upward trips might be the chances are that the dwellers in the underground world would see more of the natural world, under ecologically sounder conditions, than dwellers of surface cities do today.

I am interested to see, by the way, that the notion of underground living has begun to seem more realistic in the decades since I wrote *The Caves of Steel*. For instance, many cities in the more northerly latitudes (where cold weather, ice, and snow inhibit shopping by making it un-pleasant) are building underground shopping malls—more and more elaborate, more and more self-contained, more and more like my own imagined world.

However, my imagination is not the only one the world possesses. Here we have *Refuge*, by Rob Chilson, in which my underground city of the future is explored by another science-fiction writer skilled in his craft, who has taken my underground cities as the starting point for his own.

The stars gave no light. Derec crawled slowly along the ship's hull, peering intently through his helmet at the silvery metal. The ship was below him, or beside him, depending entirely on how one looked at it. He preferred to think of it as "beside"—he felt less as if he might fall that way.

To his left, to his right, "above" and "below" him, was nothing. But space was nothing new to Derec, whose memories began only a few months ago in a space capsule—a lifepod, in fact. At the moment he had no time for memories of the pod, of the ice asteroid, or of capture by the nonhuman pirate Aranimas. He was concentrating on swimming.

"I'm at the strut," he announced.

"Good," said Ariel, her voice booming in his helmet.

Derec hadn't time to turn his radio down, nor did he wish to let go just yet. His crawl along the hull, helped by the electromagnets in knees and palms, had been slow, but inexorable. When he seized the strut, his hand stopped but his body continued on past, like a swimmer carried by a wave. A wave of inertia.

Gripping the strut, he found himself slowly swinging around it like a flag, facing back the way he'd come. He had realized immediately that he shouldn't have grabbed the strut, but didn't compound his error by trying to undo it. He let the swing take him, absorbed his momentum with his arm—it creaked painfully—and came to a stop.

A robot, advancing in its tracks, arrested itself on the other side of the strut in the proper way: a hand braced

1

against it, the arm soaking up the momentum like a spring. Being a robot, he had no fear of sprained wrists, the most common injuries in free-fall.

The robot, Mandelbrot, paused courteously while Derec resolved his entanglement with the strut. Derec gripped it with both hands and bent one elbow while keeping the other straight. His body revolved slowly around the bent arm until he had reversed himself. Placing his foot against the strut, he tippy-toed away from it, letting go, uncoiling, and reaching out for the hull.

For a moment Derec was in free, dreamy flight, not touching the ship; then his palms touched down, the magnets clicking against it as he turned on crawlpower. He slid forward on hands and forearms while his inertia wave was absorbed by the "beach" of the ship's hull. His chest and belly and finally his knees touched down painfully, to slide scraping along.

"Frost!" said Ariel. "What are you doing, sawing the hull in half?"

Derec didn't reply. Not letting all his momentum be absorbed, he came quickly to hands and knees, reaching and pulling at the hull. The magnets were computer controlled and clicked on and off alternately in the crawl pattern.

In a few seconds he braked and all the magnets went on. He skittered slowly to a stop. Mandelbrot joined him in a similar fashion and looked at the hull, then moved aside.

"Right, we're at the hatch," said Derec. "It doesn't look like we'll need any tools to get in; just a matter of turning inset screws."

There were two slits in the hull, each in a small circle. The circles were at one edge of a square outline—the hatch. Derec stuck two fingers in one of the slits, Mandelbrot copying his motion at the other side, and they twisted the circles clockwise. There was a *pop*, and the hatch rode free.

"Got it open," Derec said.

That was a little premature. He would have to stand up on the hull to raise the hatch, or else move around. But before he could make up his mind, Mandelbrot reinserted his fingers into one of the slits and pulled. The hatch came free easily. Mandelbrot bent his arm like a rope, heaving the hatch up over his head, put up his other arm, and the hatch stood out from the hull.

"Can't see a frosted thing," muttered Derec. His helmet light bounced off the shiny underside of the hatch and again off the huddled machinery exposed, but without air to scatter the light, what he saw was a collection of parallel and crossing lines of light against velvet blackness. After a moment, however, he made out a handle. These things weren't meant only for doctorates in mechanical engineering to understand, after all. There was a release in the handle.

Squeezing the release, Derec pulled up on the handle. Nothing happened. There wasn't room on the handle for Mandelbrot to help him. Gripping it tightly, Derec stood on the hull and put his back into it. It came free with a creaky vibration he felt all the way up through the soles of his feet, an odd sort of hearing.

"Trouble?" Ariel asked, concern in her voice. Perhaps she had heard his breathing and the gasp when it broke free.

"Stuck, but I got it loose. I think a little ice had frozen around it."

With the help of the robot, who had released the hatch and now stood upright on the hull, Derec pulled out a mass of cunningly nested pipes all connected together, rather like unfolding a sofa-bed. Mandelbrot reached down and pulled a heavy cord, and a mass of thick, silvery plastic unfolded. As soon as the plastic balloon was sufficiently unfolded not to suffer damage, Derec peered down at its root.

He had to move around to the side, but there was the valve, looking uncommonly like a garden faucet on far-off Aurora. For a moment Derec was shaken by a perfect memory of a faucet in some dewy garden on the Planet of the Dawn. He'd had indications before this that he was from that greatest of Spacer planets, but very few specific memories leaked through his amnesia, fewer still were as sharp as this one.

After a few moments, though, he realized he was not

going to remember what or where that garden was. All he knew about it was that it was a pleasant memory. He had *liked* that garden. Now all he had of it was the memory of its faucet.

It isn't wise to shrug in free-fall, so Derec reached carefully inside the hatch and, bracing himself, twisted the faucet. There was a hiss he heard through his fingers and the air in the arm of his suit, as steam under low pressure rushed into the balloon. In a moment, Mandelbrot was out of sight behind it.

That wonderful flexible arm came into view, Mandelbrot twisted the return valve, and in a moment there was the faint murmur of a small pump. Water, too, was moving through the pipes by now.

The radiator and vacuum distillation sections of the water-purification-and-cooling system was in operation. They had settled down for a long stay in space.

Should have done this days ago, Derec thought but didn't say aloud. An optimist, he had hoped a ship would have come by before now. Ariel, who tended to be pessimistic, had doubted.

"I'm coming back by way of the sun side," he said. "The light's better."

Ariel didn't answer. A punch on a button made his safety line release itself and reel in from the forward airlock. He reattached it to a ring near the hatch; the robot mimicked his movements. Feeling better about standing upright on the hull, Derec strode slowly and carefully around the rather narrow cylinder until the tiny red lamp of their current "sun" came into view, then on around until it was overhead.

A class *M* dwarf, the red star was no doubt very old. It was certainly very small and it had no real planets. Its biggest daughter was an ancient lump of rock barely four hundred kilometers in diameter, its next biggest less than half that in size. Most of its daughters were fragments that ranged from respectable mountains down to fists—and there weren't many of any size. A star that old was formed at a time when the nebulas in the galaxy had only begun to be enriched with heavy elements. This was not a metalliferous star; no prospector had ever bothered to check out those lumps of rock for anything of value; none ever would.

Dim and worthless though it was, the star lit the way . . . somewhat. Under its light, the silvery hull looked like burnished copper—a pleasing sight. Shadows still were sharp-edged, his own shadow an odd-shaped, moving hole, it seemed, in the hull, a hole into some strange and otherdimensional universe.

Mandelbrot followed him gracefully.

"Detection alert," said Ariel, sounding bored. "Rock coming our way. Looks like it might be about a mouthful, if you were hungry for rocks."

"I'm not," said Derec, but it made him think of baked potatoes. He *was* getting hungry.

Had there been any danger, Ariel would have said so; Derec assumed that the rock would miss them by a wide margin. They were well out from the star, sparsely populated though its space was with junk. This was only the second thing they'd detected in two days, and the first was merely a grain of sand. Probably both objects were "dirty ice"—the stuff of comets.

Danger or no, Mandelbrot moved closer to him, scanning the sky without pausing. Derec didn't notice, and didn't bother to look for the rock. The sun drew his eye instead. At this distance, dim as it was and weak in ultraviolet light, it could be looked at directly.

Pitiful excuse though it was for a star, poor as its family was, still it made an island of light in a vast sea of darkness where stars hard and unwinking as diamonds cut at him with their stares. He thought of the space around the red star as a room, a warmly lit room in an immensity of cold and darkness.

After the circumscribed life of Robot City, he felt free. *Space,* Derec thought, *is mankind's natural home.*

There came a bark from inside the vessel, and he was reminded with a sudden chill that others than men used space. One of those others was within this ship: Wolruf, the doglike alien with whom he'd made alliance on Aranimas's ship. She had escaped first from Aranimas with him, then from the hospital station, then from Robot City.

Things had been worse for them in the past, he thought. If they had to wait here for a week or two . . .

Then he thought: *I'm worried about Ariel, though.*

He moved forward, found the airlock, and crowded in to make room for the bulky robot.

Frost condensed on his armor as soon as he entered the ship, but Derec ignored that, knowing that it wasn't too cold to touch yet; they'd only been out for minutes. It seemed even more cramped inside after having been out.

"We should spend more time outside," he said. "It's not exactly fresh air, but at least there's a feeling of freedom."

Ariel looked momentarily interested, then shrugged. "I'm all right."

Mandelbrot looked keenly at her, pausing in his ridiculous motion of scraping frost off his eyes, but said nothing. He had said nothing to Derec yet, but Derec knew that he was worried, too. Ariel had a serious disease. A fatal disease, she had said. It had caused her occasional pain before this, stabbing muscular aches, and she frequently seemed feverish and headachey and generally out of it; sometimes she even had hallucinations. But this prolonged gloom was new, and worrisome.

"So there's water for showerr, yess?" said Wolruf. She was the size of a large dog and not infrequently went on all fours, but usually walked upright, for her front paws were clumsy-seeming hands, ill-shaped by human standards but clever with tools.

"Give it half an hour," Derec said. The furry alien needed showers daily in a ship where there was no escape from each other.

"Derec, shall I prepare food?" Mandelbrot asked. "It approaches the usual hour for your meals."

Ariel roused herself, said, "I'll do that, Mandelbrot. What do you want, Derec, Wolruf?"

There were no potatoes ready. Of course he did not expect to find real food in a spaceship, and it took time for the synthesizer to prepare a specialty item. "Stew would be fine. Keep varying the mix and it'll be a long time before I get bored with it."

"I eat same as 'ou," Wolruf said.

"Borscht today," said Ariel with a smile that seemed natural. "We've got lots of tomato sauce, and besides, I like it."

"It's wonderful to have a commercial synthesizer and a large stock of basics," Derec said, cheering at her cheer. "Remember our experiments in Robot City?"

She made a face. "Remember? I'm trying to forget."

Dr. Avery's ship was well-equipped. Indeed, they could live indefinitely out here—at least until the micropile gave out, or their air and water leaked away. The water purifier used yeast and algae to reclaim sewage, the plants then being stored as basic organic matter for the synthesizer.

Derec, having removed the suit with motions suitable to a contortionist, stowed it away in its clips beside the airlock. Mandelbrot immediately went to it and checked it over. Reaching to the ceiling of the cabin, Derec touched off, tippy-toed off the floor, and back off the ceiling. Called "brachiating," it was the most efficient mode of movement within a cabin in free-fall.

He turned on the receiver. It was tuned to BEACON—*local*. A calm, feminine-sounding robotic voice spoke. "Beacon Kappa Whale Arcadia. Report, please. Beacon Kappa Whale Arcadia. Report, please." Turning off the sound, Derec glumly checked the indicators. Kappa Whale was coming in on the electromagnetic band, both laser and microwave. They were getting minimal detection on the hyperwave, however.

"I don't understand it," he muttered. Ariel glanced at him over her shoulder as she floated before the cooking equipment.

Wolruf joined him. "Wass broken by Doctorr Avery, do 'ou think?"

"Sabotage? I don't know. It was picking up Kappa Whale beautifully when we took off from Robot City."

They had left the planet of robots hurriedly in this stolen ship. Dr. Avery, who had created the robots that went on to build Robot City, had been pursuing them for reasons none of them understood. Though Derec suspected that Ariel knew more about the enigmatic and less-than-sane doctor than she had said.

Once off the planet and safe from Dr. Avery, they discovered that either there were no astrogation charts in the ship, or they were well concealed in its computer. Though positronic, that was not a full-fledged positronic brain. Had it been, they could have convinced it that without the charts they would die in space. Under the First Law of Robotics, it would be unable to withhold the charts, regardless of the orders it had been given.

The First Law of Robotics states: A robot may not knowingly harm a human being, or knowingly allow a human being to come to harm.

Orders would have come merely under the Second Law, which is: A robot must obey the orders of a human being, except where this would conflict with the First Law.

But the computer was merely a more complicated calculator, incapable of the simplest robotic thought. Robotic ships with positronic brains had been tried, and had all failed, because all full-sized positronic brains were designed with the Three Laws built into them. Necessarily, they were too intent on preventing possible harm to their occupants. Since space travel is inherently unsafe, they had a tendency to go mad or to refuse to take off.

"I feel like hitting the damn computer, or kicking it," he said.

Wolruf grinned her rather frightening grin. "Ho! 'Ou think, like Jeff Leong, all machines should have place to kick?"

"Or some way to jar information loose. I'm convinced there must be charts in there somewhere—"

It was a reasonable guess. Nobody could remember all the miles of numbers that was a star chart. Charts were rarely printed out in whole, though for convenience in calculation, some sections might be. This little ship didn't have a printer. All it had—they presumed—was a recording in its memory.

But they couldn't find it.

Even that wouldn't have been too serious if the hyperwave hadn't gone out on them. Lacking charts, in orbit about Robot City, they had swept space with the hyperwave and picked up Kappa Whale Arcadia quite well. The fix was good enough to Jump toward, and they had done that. Logically, they should then have been able to pick up other beacons and hop, skip, and jump their way to anywhere in inhabited space: the fifty Spacer worlds, or the Settler worlds that Earth had recently begun to occupy.

"We're somewhere within telescopic distance of Arcadia," murmured Derec. That was a minor and distant Spacer world. But they had no idea on which side of it lay the constellation of the Whale. They knew only that this—Kappa—was the ninth-brightest star in that constellation, and that there was only one fainter, Lambda Whale. Constellations, by interstellar agreement, had, for astrogational purposes, no more than ten stars.

"Sooner or laterr a ship will come," Wolruf said reassuringly.

Sooner or later. Derec grunted.

He didn't need to have the argument repeated; it had been mostly his. When they found that, after the Jump, the hyperwave would only pick up the nearest beacon, Derec had suggested that they lie low until a ship came by, and request a copy of the astrogational charts from it. To beam a copy over would take the ship only a few minutes, and be no trouble at all.

Sooner or later.

"Soup's on, or stew in this case," Ariel said. The oven opened with an exhalation of savory steam. "We still have some of your crusty bread, Derec. I reheated it. But we'll want more later."

"It smells good," Derec said honestly. Wolruf, with even greater honesty, licked her chops and grinned. Derec had

overcome his irritation at Ariel's invasion of the male pre-
serve of the chief of cuisine, and had admitted to her that she
was a better chef than he. (Common *cooking* was robot
work, which no human admitted to doing.)

They ate in silence for a short while. The stew was served
in covered bowls, but it clung to the inner surfaces. Manipu-
lating their spoons carefully, they were able to eat without
flinging food all over the ship. At first even Ariel's appetite
was good, but she quickly lost interest.

"Do you think a ship will ever come by here?" she asked
finally, her gaze, and apparently her thought, a long way
away.

"Of course," said Derec quickly. "I admit I was too opti-
mistic. I suspect we're well out on the edge of inhabited
space; this lane is not too well traveled. But *eventually*. . . ."

"Eventually. . ." she said, almost dreamily. She seemed,
often now, in a drifting, abstracted state.

"Eventually," Derec repeated weakly.

He was too honest to try to argue her into belief. Ships
didn't *fly* from star to star like an aircraft. They Jumped,
with massive thrusts of their hyperatomic motors, going in a
direction that was at right angles to time and all three spatial
dimensions simultaneously. Since they went no-distance, it
naturally took no-time to Jump. Therefore there were no
lanes of star travel.

For safety reasons, ships Jumped from star to star; if one
was stranded for any reason, rescuers had only to chart the
route and check every star along it. And since not every star
had inhabited planets, all along these well-traveled lanes (as
they were called) were the beacon stars. A ship Jumping into
this beacon system was supposed to verify that it had indeed
arrived at Kappa Whale, beam its ship's log to the beacon's
recorders, and depart. Periodically, patrol ships copied those
records to assure that nothing untoward had happened.

But days had passed and no ships had appeared. Of
course a ship appearing on the other side of Kappa Whale
would not be detected by them on the electromagnetic band
until it had Jumped out. The hyperwave radio, though, was

functioning well enough to detect a ship reporting to the beacon anywhere in this stellar system. Derec and Wolruf agreed on that.

So: eventually they would be found and rescued.

Wolruf finished her meal by opening her bowl and licking it clean efficiently. "I wass thinking," she said. "Maybe Jump-wave shock shifted things in 'ou'rr hyperwave antenna."

"Shifted the elements?" Derec nodded uncertainly. He had no idea where he had been educated, but he had a good general technical background with a strong specialty in robotics—not unusual for a Spacer youth, as he assumed himself to be. But hyperwave technology was a whole other and, if anything, even more difficult school of knowledge.

"Do 'ou have—'ou know—things to measure them with?"

Derec had seen a toolbox on the ship's schematic that he had accessed before going out to set up the recycling system. "There might be."

There was. A few minutes later, with Ariel listless at the detectors and Wolruf at the communicator, Derec carefully strode forward outside, followed by Mandelbrot.

The hyperwave antenna could have been put in any part of the ship, since the hyperatomo didn't kowtow to the laws of space-time, but it would have had to have been well shielded lest its backlash in the small ship damage the instruments, or even the crew. So in these Star Seeker models it was in a blister on the bow, as far from everything as possible.

The antenna looked like a series of odd-shaped chunks of metal and coils of wire, and the testing gear simply shot current through each element in turn. The readouts were within normal range, as nearly as he could tell from the manual he had accessed before coming out.

"I don't get it," Derec complained, thinking of the classical definition of Hell: the place where all the instruments test out to be perfect, but none of them work. "How can I fix it if it isn't broken?"

"I think," said Wolruf slowly, "that Dr. Avery hass re-tuned the antenna."

"Retuned?" Derec had never heard of such a thing, but knew little about the subject. "I thought all Spacer talk was in the same range. Is he trying to pick up—Settlers? Or what?"

"Maybe Aranimass."

Maybe, Derec thought, chilled. *Maybe, indeed.* That long-armed pirate was definitely interested in Dr. Avery's doings, though he might not know who or what Dr. Avery was.

Derec stood, looking around the warm room generated by Kappa Whale, and shivered. For the first time the thought came to him: *What if the first ship that showed up was Aranimas's? He must be systematically searching the beacon stars—*

A touch on his arm nearly made Derec jump off the hull.

The burnished, enigmatic face of Mandelbrot approached his. The robot gripped him with his normal left arm. His Avery-construct right arm bent impossibly, reached around Derec and switched off his communicator.

Derec had had nightmares about that arm. It was a piece of scrap from an Avery robot, which Aranimas had had picked up from the ice asteroid where Derec had first awakened. "Build me a robot," the alien had said. Derec had put pieces together to build the robot he called Alpha. It wasn't a good job, but it worked.

Then, weeks later, the crudely attached right arm seated itself firmly and made a few modifications in Alpha's brain: Alpha informed them that he was now known as Mandelbrot. Derec had observed the fine structure of the arm: a series of tiny chips, or scales, that gripped each other and could therefore mold the arm to any shape that might be desired.

Each unit was a sort of robotic cell; together, they were a brain. And having integrated themselves, they had—to a degree—taken over Alpha. Derec's nightmare was that the cells were *eating* the robot out from the inside, that his interior was one solid mass of them, and he was about to become something—horrifying.

Impossible; the cells couldn't eat. Also, all the brains were robotic, Mandelbrot's normal positronic brain and the units in the cells. The Three Laws compelled them all. But dreams are not logical.

At the moment, the worst nightmare had come true, until Mandelbrot put his head against Derec's helmet. It would have looked to an observer as if the robot were kissing his cheek: his microphone touched Derec's helmet and Mandelbrot spoke.

"Derec, I am worried about Ariel."

They had been careful to conceal from Mandelbrot the worst of Ariel's condition. The robot knew only that she was sick, not that the disease was usually fatal. The effect on his positronic brain was more than they cared to risk; the First Law left no loophole for incurable diseases.

"Ariel is bored, as well as ill," Derec said.

He looked away uneasily from the robot's expressionless but intense face. The stars beckoned, promising and threatening; somewhere out there, perhaps, he might recover his memory. He remembered Jeff Leong, who had crashed on Robot City after an accident while on his way to college. In a few years, Derec would have been thinking about college, if this fantastic thing hadn't happened to him.

"Ariel is very sick," said Mandelbrot. "Her eating pattern has altered markedly. She suffers from fever most of the time. Her attention span is abnormally low, she is sensitive to light, she moves about only with effort—"

"All right," said Derec, feeling that he would ossify before the robot finished its catalog if he didn't interrupt. "It's true that Ariel is ill. But I am not worried about her."

That wasn't true, especially now that it had been brought out into the open.

"You should worry. I fear for her safety if something is not done for her."

"What do you suggest we do?"

"You may have to use the Key to Perihelion."

After scouring Robot City for weeks for a Key to Perihelion, the mysterious device that would transport them instantly off the planet, they had managed to steal Dr. Avery's ship when he had come to investigate their "interference." On the ship they had found the Key, but Derec's investiga-

tion of Dr. Avery's office had shown him where the Key
would probably take him.

Derec said, "That would take us back to Robot City—
with no way of escape and Dr. Avery after us. Surely that's
less safe than this mild illness."

Mandelbrot was silent for a moment. Then he said, "That
is true. I hope you are right and that this is a mild illness.
But she has suffered many of these symptoms for many days
now. Mild illnesses usually subside within this time."

The robot fell silent but did not move away.

"'Ou might as well come back in," said Wolruf, startling
Derec. "I do not think we can find the problem out therre. I
wish I knew more about dense energy fieldss. . . ."

Derec turned, and at his first motion the robot released
him, first turning his communicator back on. The motion
was as much an indicator of Derec's will as a command, and
the Second Law of Robotics forced the robot to comply with
his desire.

"Right, I'm coming back," Derec said, as if there had
been no hiatus in their communications.

He returned reluctantly. There was free-fall within the
cabin—and three times as much space as there had been
under acceleration—but there were decks and bulkheads and
overheads. Out here he was in his element. It was like floating in warm salt water. Even the cumbersome suit didn't
detract from the feeling of freedom he got from letting his
gaze rove out and on out, from star to ever-more-distant star.
All of them waiting, just beyond this red-lit room.

Stars beyond stars, with their waiting worlds, which now
only the Earth Settlers were opening up. And beyond, other
intelligent races, other adventures. . . . A member of one of
those races waited now in the ship. Derec had again a moment of intense wonder that he of all people should be
among the first to meet aliens. Most of those who had met
the pirate Aranimas hadn't survived. . . .

Who knew what other beings awaited them among all
those bright stars? He wondered why the Spacers had sat for

so many centuries on their fifty worlds, too satisfied to go looking for adventure. The way he felt now, it was impossible to believe.

Derec had an impulse to jump and go tumbling head under heels across the sky, but he knew Ariel would think it silly with his safety line and dangerous without. *Right on both counts,* he thought ruefully. *Frost, why can't I be a little kid for once? I can't remember ever having been one; it's like I've been cheated out of all that kiddish fun....*

There was a warm, pleasant smell in the air of the ship when they reentered. "I made toast," said Ariel emptily.

She had toasted the last of the crusty bread, but hadn't buttered it. It was now nearly cold. Derec pretended not to notice, merely nodded and thanked her, trying to sound pleased. Popping the slices into the oven, he reheated them, and punched up his sequence for bread on the synthesizer—three loaves. When the toast was warmed, he buttered it and shared it with Wolruf. The caninoid, like a true dog, was always ready to eat, if only a bite or two.

Ariel wasn't hungry.

"I think Doctorr Avery hass retuned the hyperwave antenna by changing the densities of the force-fieldss in the core elementss," Wolruf said, exhaling crumbs. "Dense force-fieldss arre the only things that can stop hyperatomos. But why change it, if not to detect something?"

Derec nodded uncertainly. A dense force-field was one that permeated some object; a magnet with a keeper across its poles was the classic example. Altering the density of the atomic-level fields in the core elements of the antenna would change the "acceptance" of the core.

"If not to detect something, like, say, Aranimas's ship or transmissions?" he asked. "It's a consideration. It's not unlikely that they have crossed paths, as Dr. Avery has Keys to Perihelion and Aranimas wants them."

It might well be reassuring, then, that the hyperwave wasn't detecting anything. It might mean that Aranimas wasn't operating anywhere around here.

"Ariel, you seem sleepy," said Mandelbrot. "It approaches your usual bedtime. Perhaps you should go to bed."

"Yes, good idea," said Ariel vaguely. She continued to sit and stare vacantly for another fifteen minutes before sighing deeply and getting slowly "up".

When she had gone to the one private cabin the little ship boasted, Wolruf turned fiercely on Derec.

"She iss sick! 'Ou must do something, Derec! The robot iss worried. I am worried."

Mandelbrot had accompanied Ariel into the cabin. Derec lowered his voice, nevertheless. "You're right. Don't let Mandelbrot know how far advanced her condition is; it might destroy his brain."

Wolruf caught his breath. "She will die? Iss that what you mean?"

Derec nodded, haggard. "She told me her disease is usually fatal. I-I'd been hoping that it wouldn't be. But since we've been sitting here, doing nothing. . . ."

"I think some iss boredom. But mosst is sickness!"

Derec nodded. The cabin door opened and Mandelbrot emerged, closed it gently, and moved purposefully toward them, fingers against the overhead, toes against the deck.

"Ariel must have medical attention," he said bluntly when he was close, speaking as circumspectly as Derec and Wolruf had done. "The First Law demands it. I fear for her life if this trend continues, Derec."

They looked at him and he saw it coming.

"You must use the Key to Perihelion."

Wolruf nodded her agreement.

Derec felt sick at the thought of returning to Robot City, even aside from the thought of Dr. Avery. "That would leave you here with no spacesuit and only Mandelbrot able to go outside—"

"Iss no matter. 'Ou musst not rissk Ariel'ss life."

"It is a First Law imperative." Mandelbrot could not conceive that a human could resist that imperative, any more than he himself could.

"Very well. As soon as she has awakened and eaten. Tomorrow, in other words. And I hope Dr. Avery isn't at home."

The thing that alarmed Derec most next morning was that Ariel didn't resist. A tart-tongued young woman, had she been in her normal condition she'd have frosted them well. As it was, there was a spark of eagerness in her eye, not so much, Derec thought, hope that the robotic Human Medical Team on Robot City might have found a cure, as relief from boredom.

It was no small risk they were taking. Dr. Avery was brilliant, a genius, but undoubtedly insane—megalomaniacal. Humans were but robots to him, to be used as he wished.

Derec looked at Ariel.

Frost, he thought, *I hope we make it.* She had come to mean a lot to him. How much, he hadn't been free to say. She did, after all, have this disease. It was not readily contagious, and in fact Derec had learned that it was sexually transmitted. Additionally, she remembered him from before his memory began.

Apparently there had once been some kind of strong emotion between them, and she was torn two ways by the memory, or by the contrast between his present innocent state and what had once been between them. She had told him frustratingly little about himself, though he thought she knew much.

None of her secretiveness mattered. She was Ariel, and he would rather be sick himself than see her suffer so.

Nevertheless, going back to Robot City was a wrench when they'd come so near to escaping.

"We might as well get it over with," said Ariel. He thought she sounded better than she had for days. Possibly being chased halfway across Robot City would be good for her.

Mandelbrot handed Derec the Key. It was rectangular and flat, small enough to hold in a hand, but larger than any mechanical key. It glittered in the light, looking more like silver than aluminum. It was in fact a highly conductive alloy permeated with a force-field. That made it more reflective than any unenergized metal, and was suggestive of hyperatomics.

Derec put an arm around Ariel for stability and pressed the Key into her palm, gripping her hand from below. As both of them gripped the Key, he pressed each corner in turn. Derec considered that the Keys had a nonhuman source, though the robots on Robot City had learned to make them. Humans wouldn't design a control system like that.

When the fourth corner was pressed, a button rose from the smooth, seamless surface. Derec took a final glance around, nodded farewell to the caninoid and the robot, and to the ship itself. There wasn't time for lengthy speeches; the button would soon recede.

He pressed the button.

The ship disappeared from around them, and fog took its place.

Perihelion.

The word meant the point in an orbit closest to a sun— more accurately, *the* sun, the Sun of old Earth. But now the term was synonymous with periastron. Perihelion had been described to them as the place closest to every place else in the universe.

They retained their floating attitudes, still in free fall, and looked around. Perihelion hadn't changed. All around them was a soft gray light, and air, air that smelled fuggy and dusty. No purifiers here, thought Derec, twisting to look around. It seemed that Perihelion went on forever, but he suspected that it had sharp limits to its size.

"What are you looking for?" Ariel asked, sounding as if she cared again.

"The hyperatomic motors."

"The what?"

"The Jump motors. This Key couldn't have brought us here by itself, not if the robots could duplicate it. It has to be tuned to motors elsewhere; I think it's just a tiny hyperwave radio. I don't know if we're in hyperspace or if this is a place in normal space—a big balloon, the size of a planet, perhaps."

"You mean, somebody *made* it?" Ariel asked, aghast.

"It's obviously an alien transport station—maybe for moving really heavy freight," said Derec. "It may be one of many. I wonder if it's abandoned, or if it's actually in use but is so big we don't see the others and they don't see us."

"The light comes from all sides," Ariel said, thoughtfully.

"Yes," said Derec, also thoughtful. "I hadn't thought of that. Well, much remains mysterious. It would take a small ship to explore this place."

In any case, they could do nothing now.

"We might as well get on with it," said Ariel, bored once the first interest had worn off. She made a face at the thought of Robot City, but Derec was heartened. She hadn't had that much spirit last night.

Derec repeated the keying motions and pressed the button. Gravity slapped their feet and light slapped their eyes. They looked around in shock. Walls surrounded them—obviously the walls of an apartment. But this wasn't an apartment designed by Avery robots. They weren't on Robot City.

They had no idea where they were.

The apartment was small, cramped, mean. It had not been lived in—there were no human touches, no pictures of relatives, no flowers or personalized decorations. It was very clean, but the flooring looked worn—no carpets—and the door handles looked dulled from use. A silly-looking robot stood against one wall.

This room was perhaps three meters by five and had a chair and a small couch that might seat two—three if they didn't mind contact. There was a curious blank space against one wall; a control panel was near one closed door. An open door led into what seemed to be a bedroom. A third door was closed and smaller than the others.

In the bedroom, Derec saw when he took a step, was another closed door. It was side by side with the closed door in this room, and he judged that they were both closets. Also in that wall, in both rooms, were drawer pulls—drawers built into the wall. A faint mechanical hum permeated the apartment.

And that was it.

"Just two rooms," he said in disbelief.

"No bathroom!" said Ariel.

"No. And no kitchen or dining room."

They looked at each other. The only thing Derec could think of was a prison, but that wasn't right; there'd be a bathroom, at least. And this was too small and sterile for a prison, anyway.

"I wonder if that robot is functional," said Ariel, frowning at it.

It didn't *look* functional. It had a rigid, silly grin on a plastic face, unlike any robot Derec had seen or heard of. Now that he looked at it critically, its joints and the associated drive mechanisms looked large and clumsy. His training in robotics had dealt primarily with the brains, but the bodies, too, had been covered. It seemed to be looking at them, but it hadn't moved, of course.

"Robot, are you functional?" Derec asked.

"Yes, master," it said obsequiously, not moving, that fatuous grin never altering.

Robots should not have phoney human faces, Derec thought in irritation; one kept wanting to respond, but there was no emotion there to respond to.

"What is your name?"

"My name is R. David, master."

Ariel looked questioningly at him. Derec shook his head. Robots often had human names, if they attended humans. Ariel had told him that as a child she had named her nurse robot Guggles, though her parents had named the robot Katherine. Nowhere, though, had he heard of a robot with a prefix to its name. R. David? Or had he heard—

"R. David, what planet is this?" Ariel asked.

"This is Earth, Miss Avery," the robot said respectfully.

Startled—staggered, in fact—they looked at each other. Of course! The rooms were so small, so cramped and mean, because Earth was immensely overpopulated. It had more people than all fifty Spacer worlds put together. The robot was crude because Earthmen were backward in robotics and in fact had a strong prejudice against them.

As strong as their prejudice against Spacers.

"We might have been better off back on Robot City," Derec said.

"Maybe we can get back to civilization from here," Ariel said.

"Good thinking. R. David, is it possible to take ship from Earth to the Spacer worlds?"

"Yes, Mr. Avery. Ships leave Earth at least weekly, and often more frequently."

Mr. Avery! And he had called Ariel "Miss Avery." They glanced at each other and with one accord decided not to mention it.

It seemed obvious to Derec that this robot was accustomed to seeing Dr. Avery come and go in the instantaneous fashion possible only to Key wielders. It had accepted that "Avery" could come and go in such fashion. Seeing them arrive in the same way, it came to the logical but wrong conclusion that they were "Averys," though they were obviously not "Dr. Avery."

"The first thing to do, then, is to get to the spaceport," Derec said. "Does that door lead to the outside?"

"One moment, Mr. Avery, if you please. It would not be wise for you to venture forth without preparation."

"What sort of preparation?" Derec asked. The robot was right; this *was* Earth.

"First, you will need a complete prophylactic regimen against the diseases of Earth. These are many and varied, and you have no natural immunity."

Frost, that was so. They looked at each other in alarm.

"However, the problem is not so great as most Spacers believe."

The robot stirred, opened a drawer in the wall and produced hypoguns, vials, pills. Grimacing, but needing no urging, they submitted themselves to their use.

"Take the pills when next you drink. If at any time you have any physical sensations of illness, you must notify me at once. It will be necessary to diagnose you immediately for treatment."

Derec and Ariel nodded solemnly, more than a little nervous at the thought of Earthly diseases.

"You will also need identification, ration slips and tags, and money," said R. David decisively when that was done. Moving clumsily, it opened the door to the closet in the sitting room. It was jammed with things, from a bookviewer and boxes of records to compact duplication devices.

Derec recognized these as Spacer-made, and surmised that it would be no great feat to duplicate Earthly ID symbols.

In this he was correct. R. David lowered the blank thing on the wall—a folding table—and spent an hour or so producing numerous bits of plastic and metal bearing their pictures, long numbers, various obscure statements about them, and of course a complete ID workup, including fingerprints, footprints, retinal scans, corneal images, ear pictures, and blood analysis.

"Dr. Avery procured comparatively large sums of Earthly money when he first landed," R. David explained. "He traded rare metals for it. Of course, money as such is of little value on Earth, as it can only be used to purchase nonessentials such as book recordings. Food, housing, clothing, and so on, are rationed."

"Frost," said Ariel nervously. "I wouldn't want some poor Earther to starve because I got his rations."

"There is no danger of that, Miss Avery. There is ample margin. It does no harm to anyone to provide you with Earthly ID, as Dr. Avery has more than paid for the consumption of Earth's scarce resources with his rare metals. Rationed items are available in amounts and qualities controlled by the individual's rating."

"Rating?"

"One's position in Earthly society. I understand that things are not greatly different in any human society, but on Earth such things have been formalized to a much higher degree."

"It's true that in the Spacer worlds the most important people usually get the best of what's going," said Ariel wryly. "Maybe Earth is actually more honest in admitting this. What kind of government does Earth have? Is it democratic, aristocratic, or what? Do the higher ratings run everything?"

"In answer to your last question, yes, to a degree. Earth is a democratic syndicalism, with elections to Parliament made from location—in the lower house—and from industry to the upper house, or senate. Elections are democratic in those areas, but most of the administration is by appointed officials, these being people who have passed certain tests and worked their way up from less important offices. Syndicalism means that industry—primarily the feeding, housing, and clothing of the population—dominates the government."

"I can see how that would be necessary," said Derec, watching the robot's big, clumsy hands proceed delicately at their task. "How many ratings are there, and what's the highest?"

"Currently there are twenty-one ratings. The rating *A* is usually considered the highest. It is rarely bestowed. Only ten million humans are in this rating category."

One out of ten, Derec thought automatically. Then he caught himself. No: on Aurora, or most of the Spacer worlds, ten million would be ten percent of the populace. But Earth had—

"What's the population of Earth, R. David?" Ariel asked, having paralleled Derec's thought.

"Eight billion, Miss Avery."

Eight billion! They looked at each other. The population of eighty Spacer worlds—and there were only fifty.

"Who is in the *A* rating? Government officials?"

"No, this rating is reserved for entrepreneurs who solve large problems, for inventors, heroic spacemen, and other adventurers. It may be conferred by popular acclaim, as in the case of certain beloved entertainers. Recipients of the *A* rating have many privileges, among them the right to adorn their doors with laurel."

A high honor, like the Medal of Aurora. Derec nodded; the details—what was laurel?—didn't matter.

"What's the next lowest rating?"

"*B* rating is reserved for planetary and continental governmental officials, both elected and appointed. *C* refers to City officials. *D* is for industry officials. From there it becomes complex and not obvious. There are fifteen steps in each rating, the lowest being step one."

"So, what rate and step are you preparing for us?"

"I am preparing identification for T ratings, as I did for Dr. Avery, as I assume you will wish to remain anonymous as Spacers. It will certainly facilitate your investigations of Earthly society if you pass unremarked, and the T rating is the best for that purpose."

"What kind of people normally are assigned T ratings?" Ariel asked.

"The 'T' stands for 'Transient.' Any person whose duties require him or her to travel may be assigned this rating, unless the rating itself allows of that eventuality, as do B ratings and many A ratings. Salesmen, for instance, may be rated D or $T,$ but usually $T,$ as D is assigned to administrative duties.

"In your cases," R. David continued, "I had considered assigning you S ratings—students—but I judged it not advisable, as students have certain restrictions, and I would be forced to specify a school."

Interesting as all this was, Derec found the hour it took to prepare the ID dragging. The tiny-roomed apartment, with only two rooms, was a prison more confining than any he had viewed in historical novels. Even the dungeons of the ancient times on Earth had seemed larger. The varying mechanical drone seemed to grow louder and louder until he was forced to speak, whereupon it faded at once to its actual low level.

It was the sound, he thought in some awe, of the City—a sound no Earthman could avoid, from birth to death. For they never went outside their Cities.

Finally, the ID was completed, and R. David explained the uses of the various pieces. "This is your ration tag for food; your home kitchen is 9-G. Personals are also assigned, but you may use any you see. Derec, take care not to speak to or look at anyone in Personal; there is a strong taboo for men on Earth. Ariel, women have no such taboo; you may speak in Personal. Your ratings do not grant you stall privileges. You must supply your own combs, brushes, and shaving equipment."

R. David droned on, provided them with a map of the

local area. There was an attempt to put everything on the same level, they learned. Their quarters were low-status, and so they had to go up or down to Personals and commissary.

At length the robot gave them hats and let them go, obviously worried. Ariel opened the door and stepped out, Derec following.

The same oyster-white walls as the interior; they might have been in a very cheap hotel, and in fact, Derec surmised, they were. A youth with long, elaborately coiffed hair and gaudy cheap clothes gave them a sullen look from down the corridor as he entered an apartment. An older woman, heavy and squarish and short, passed them, carrying an open bottle and exhaling the odor of mousey beer. She did not so much not look at them as not see them.

Turning to the right, Derec led them toward a gleam of brighter light. Behind them, two men exited from an apartment, talking casually together about a sports event, oddly called "boxing." Moments later, Derec and Ariel were at the junction.

A wider, busier corridor crossed theirs at right angles. Ariel pointed out the sign that told them that theirs was Sub-Corridor 16. They had just entered Corridor M. Turning left, they followed a small crowd, which quickly resolved itself into an accidental grouping. There must have been fifty people in view at any given moment, Derec estimated, and was slightly staggered.

Abruptly, on the right the wall became transparent and they looked into an open space in which children raced about and bounced balls. A playground. The inside of the wall had crude bits of childish art affixed to it; posters boasted of obscure triumphs, and "recitations" were advertised. It was strange, yet Derec found it familiar. Sometime in his forgotten past he had played in such a playground, though nothing specific came through.

One thing, though, he missed: the gleam of attentive robots along the wall and amid the yelling mobs.

Corridor M terminated at a large circular junction. In the

angles, four escalator strips spiraled—two up and two down. Beyond, according to the signs, was another subsection: theirs was Sub-Section G.

Perhaps a hundred men, women, and children were visible, Derec thought. He and Ariel, awed, slowed their pace and drifted to one side of the center of the junction, avoiding both the mouths of the corridors and the escalators. A hundred—and not the same hundred. Moment by moment, people filtered in and filtered out, up or down, away along the corridors, or in from either direction.

Derec supposed wildly that within ten minutes a person might see—oh—five hundred people. Frost! Maybe a thousand!

And now that the playground had alerted him, he noted that none of them were robots.

There were small tables with uncomfortable-looking benches before them, at which people sat, some playing chess. Other benches without tables, equally uncomfortable in appearance, harbored other people. Not far from them an old fellow like a wrinkled apple smiled cherubically at everything he saw; beside him on the bench was an uncapped bottle wrapped in brown paper up to the neck. Others who sat about were also old. Some played chess or other board games at the tables; some snacked on various foodstuffs.

The walls under the escalators had identifying marks high up, but lower down there were large boards with papers affixed to them, announcing various events. Below that still were wide strips running from escalator to corridor mouth, on which crude, vigorous murals had been painted. At one corner an earnest group of youths, younger than Ariel or Derec, were touching the mural lightly with flat applique boards, painting a new mural over the old. Watching them was a young woman all in blue. She looked short, square, sturdy, and wore an odd cap with a bill of translucent blue that threw a blue shadow over her face; above the bill was a golden medal.

She turned and they saw that she had the label C-3 on her

upper left chest, and a tool of some sort dangling from her left side: it was half a meter long and had a sturdy grip. *C* ratings were City functionaries, Derec remembered. Then he realized that the tool was a neuronic whip. No; it was far too big and heavy; the neuronic whip might be in that buttoned-shut pouch in front. The tool had to be a club.

A policewoman. Her eye took them in, paused, went on, and she crossed to speak to one of the old parties at a table. Derec stared in fascination. He had never, to his knowledge, laid eyes on one whose duty was to apply force to other human beings.

"Standing here as we are, we stand out; she's probably trained to notice people who act oddly," Ariel said in a low voice.

Derec agreed wordlessly, started toward the down escalator, reflecting that no one could understand them from a little distance if they spoke normally, so great was the noise of people and the murmur of the escalators.

Each escalator flattened out where it met the floor, and there was a three-meter strip of level surface. Ahead of them, Earthmen strode forward and stepped on without breaking stride, then turned about to face their direction of travel. Derec and Ariel tried to imitate that confident stride. At least the example taught them to enter against the direction of travel, a thing Derec wouldn't have guessed. They stepped on with only a slight flexing of the legs and a quick shuffle to retain balance. They turned around and looked down, just as the strip dived down behind the wall.

The escalator, they saw, was not actually a stairway, as they had expected; it was a flat, moving ramp. Overhead was a sloping ceiling from which came the muted rumble of drives; one of the other strips, Derec supposed, probably an up strip. The down escalator did a complete half-circle clockwise, then the wall to their right opened and they were on the other side of the junction at the next level down.

One more half-circle, another junction, then there came a full circle with no exit, and they were at the bottom. The murmur became thunderous. The escalator dived into a slit in the floor, and, Derec presumed, ran "underground" for a few meters, only to reverse itself and climb backward, out of the floor and up. There were only two strips, not four, each going both up and down simultaneously.

Two dozen people got off below them, then they got off, and fifty more followed them, dispersing briskly in all directions, fighting through hundreds of people going eight different ways. This junction was four times as busy as the ones they'd seen above. Derec and Ariel tried not to gape.

Light and noise came through the arches that replaced the corridor mouths above, and they saw people whirling past. If before they'd seen hundreds, now they saw thousands!

Derec swallowed a small knot of fear. So many people! He got the distinct impression he'd never seen that many people together before. He realized he was making quick calculations of how much air they were using, and, more importantly, how much was left for him. *No,* he thought, *if there's enough for eight billion, there's enough for me.*

To right and left, moving strips hurtled past, faster and faster and higher and higher as they got farther from the junction. High overhead were glowing, crawling signs like worms of light, the largest saying WEBSTER GROVES. Before and behind them, the other two arches opened on the non-moving space between the strips. It was dotted with kiosks—some being communications booths, some being the heads of strips that came up from below. Far away down the concourse was another wide tube coming down from the ceiling, with its four escalators. Behind, at the limits of sight, was another.

They drifted out, read the signs, awed. People swarmed about them, the noise was continuous and not so loud as it seemed, the air was warm and humid and thick with the odor of thousands, hundreds of thousands, of people.

"So this is Earth."

CHAPTER 4

THERE'S NO PLACE LIKE HOME-KITCHEN

Hesitantly, Derec led the way to the expressway that ran west, as it proclaimed. The lightworms overhead proclaimed KIRKWOOD EXITS NEXT.

They mounted the first strip. It was traveling at about half walking speed, and each succeeding strip was that much faster than the previous. A fat old man skipped nimbly across three strips in a practiced motion that would have sent Derec tumbling. Sedately, he and Ariel crossed three strips, then she gasped and gripped his arm.

Hurriedly they recrossed the strips, going down, and were carried only a little way past their destination. They had gotten nowhere near the fast lanes of the express.

Once between the ways again they were a little puzzled, but there was a kiosk not far away, from which people emerged. Entering it, they found strips to carry them down to a cross-corridor that would take them under the ways. They surfaced on the other side of the express strips, where there was a set of localways, rode the second-slowest strip back for a short distance and got off, to dive into a huge corridor.

It was lined with shops of various kinds, but they didn't stop to look. Thousands of people were peering through the transparent walls at bright displays of goods.

At the second cross-corridor was the symbol for the Personal. It wasn't the one to which they were assigned; they must have passed that within minutes after leaving the apartment. At Ariel's questioning look, Derec nodded, but he felt a qualm though he walked firmly toward the door to the Men's Personal. For the first time, they were separated.

Don't look at or speak to anyone, R. David had said. He pushed open the door and found himself in an anteroom. No one lingered there, so he also passed on, through a door ingeniously arranged not to be in line of sight of the first. Inside he saw a series of small hallways lined with blank doors, about half with red lights glowing. Some of these little cubicles were four times as large as others, and as a man exited one he glimpsed such felicities as laundry facilities. The stalls, he supposed, to which he had no access.

The tiny cubicle his keyed plastic strip got him into had a crude john, a metal mirror, and below it a wash basin. There was no towel, merely a device to blow hot, dry air. The showers were at the other end.

He felt better when he left. After a lengthy wait, Ariel reappeared, looking radiant.

Derec stared. Certainly she was looking better than she had in days on shipboard. He had a wild hope that she was not really sick after all, or that she had experienced one of those mysterious remissions that still baffled doctors. Then he realized that he was letting his wishes rule his reason, and cursed himself for setting himself up for a reaction.

"Shall we go?" she asked, smiling and taking his arm.

It was not far to the section kitchen to which they were assigned. As T-4s they could go to any kitchen they happened to be near, but that would entail accounting difficulties for the staff of the kitchen, and might draw attention to them.

Three lines of people formed up at the door, right, left, and center. They joined one of the lines, readying their metal ration tags. Ahead of them the Earthers—talking and laughing uninhibitedly, as was their wont—filtered forward, inserting their tags into slots and after a moment recovering them and striding into noisy confusion, removing their hats. There was a strong, pleasant odor of unfamiliar food.

"Hey, Charlie!" came a raucous cry from behind them, making them jump a little. Someone in the line behind them had recognized someone in the next line. "Back from Yeast Town, hey?"

Charlie answered incomprehensibly, something about being good to be back. "Right!" bellowed the man behind them. "No kitchen like home-kitchen, eh?"

Considering that they all must serve food from the same source, Derec thought, that must just be familiarity, not the food. Come to think of it, if everybody ate in such kitchens three times a day, they'd soon get to know their neighbors at the nearby tables.

They moved forward, Derec's tag slippery in his hand. With nothing better to do, he counted the people passing through the entry. Each line filtered diners through at about one per second. Sixty per minute. At least a hundred and eighty per minute for the three lines. *Frost!* he thought. *And we've been in line for five minutes!*

It got worse; something like eighteen hundred people must have entered in the ten minutes it took them to work their way to the entry. A turnstile barred their way. Derec boldly thrust his tag into the slot of the machine. It blinked at him (non-positronic computer, he thought), lit up with the legend TABLE J-9/NO FREE CHOICE, and ejected the tag. Derec took it and found that the turnstile gave under pressure from his knee. Ariel followed in a moment, but there was no time to breathe easily.

Beyond stretched an enormous room.

The whole City was one gigantic steel and concrete cavern, and this was the largest opening in it that they had seen, except for the slash of the moving ways. It went on, it seemed, forever. From the ceiling, which glowed coolly, descended pillars in an orderly array, short sections of transparent wall (apparently to minimize noise) and columns apparently full of tubes and cables. Between them stretched the tables—kilometers of tables, in ranks and files. All was confusion, and the Earthers were swarming past them while they stood gaping: the gleam of light on polished imitation wood, the clatter of plastic flatware on plastic plates, the babble of thousands of voices, the crying of children. Behind manual windows to their right and left, men and women dealt with those whose feeding could not be automated.

Overhead, light-signs indicated the rows, and at Ariel's nudge Derec started the long trudge to row J.

Because of his Spacer conditioning, he had been thinking of this kitchen as a Spacer restaurant, with maybe a dozen tables, most for four people, some for two, a few for eight or ten. But these tables each seated—he guessed fifty on each side. Even after they reached row J, table 9 was a long way away.

Hesitantly, they approached it—at least it was plainly marked—and found two seats together. The people they passed were grumbling because choice was suspended. "Too many transients," growled someone, and they felt guilty.

"Food is probably one of the few high spots of their days," Ariel whispered.

They took their seats and looked at the raised section of the table before them.

NO FREE CHOICE glowed to the right. On the left was a panel that said: *Chicken—Sundays, opt. Mon. Fish—Fridays, opt. Sat.* On Earth, there was a seven-day week, but Derec had no idea which day was which. There being no choice, he shrugged, glanced at Ariel, and pressed the contact. The panel immediately lit with: *Zymosteak: Rare, Med., Well-D?* Not Sunday or Friday, he thought. Derec chose well-done and the sign vanished, replaced with *Salad: Tonantzin, Calais, Del Fuego, PepperTom?*

Ariel shrugged, glancing at him, and they chose, suppressing smiles; neither had heard of any of these dressings.

ORDER PLACED.

That sign stared at them for several minutes. The Earthmen around them were a scruffy lot, and Derec realized that he had been subliminally aware of that for some time. Earthers were short, and tended to be plain, if not actually homely. Here and there a handsome man or a beautiful woman attracted admiring glances, but they were a minority.

At least Earth people weren't starving, as Derec had expected. He knew vaguely that it took a major effort on the part of the population and its robots—restricted to the countryside—to feed Earth. Standard food synthesizers were too expensive, and used much too much energy for Earth to afford. But a large minority of these people were fat, and many more were plump. ·

At this table they waited patiently, not talking or laughing as at other tables.

"Probably a table for Transients who don't know each other," Ariel said, low-toned. There were only a couple of quiet conversations at the table.

Presently, the food ended their embarrassment; a disk slid aside in front of each of them and another rose into position, the second one holding a covered server of plastic. When they removed the servers from the service disks, the latter closed smoothly.

The food looked like steak, baked potato with shrimp sauce, and a salad with dressing on the side. Crusty, faintly yellow bread. It smelled marvelous and, to Derec's amazement, it was natural. His first bite confirmed that: the rich, subtle, varied flavor of real food was unmistakable. And yet it wasn't real food, either. Zymosteak? It was plain these people normally got meat only twice a week, with a chance at it on two more days. Four days out of seven.

"I can't believe it's so good," Ariel said under the cover of the clatter of Earthers opening their servers.

Derec hadn't realized he was so hungry; it hadn't been that long since breakfast. Perhaps he'd gotten so bored with synthetic food that he'd been eating less and less.

He turned his attention to another problem. They had been served with amazing rapidity. He couldn't remember service on any Spacer world, but he was sure it wasn't this fast. There had to be automation behind the scenes. Of course, with no free choice, they had merely to drop the chosen kind of dressing into the server, clamp the lid down, and pop it into an oven for the few seconds required to cook the zymosteak to the desired degree. Probably ran it through the oven on a belt. With a good oven, there could have been ice cream on the same plate and it wouldn't have melted before the meat was done.

Even so, row J was the last: ten rows of ten tables each; a hundred tables, each seating a hundred. This commissary was equipped to feed ten thousand people. Derec mentioned as much to Ariel, who was as dumbfounded as he. It wasn't at capacity now; perhaps there were *only* six thousand people in the room.

On Aurora, a sports arena that seated ten thousand was a big one.

Halfway through the meal, Derec found his breath coming fast: it was too much. He felt trapped in this concrete cavern, felt that the spacious room was closing in, the ceiling, not low but not high, was the lid of a trap, the mobs of unconscious people around him weren't real. *They probably went all their lives without seeing the sun or open air,* he thought, and that made it worse. With difficulty, he fought off the panic, panting.

When they had finished their meals, they put the servers and flatware back on the disk and pressed the same contact again, as they'd seen their neighbors do, and watched them vanish. The exit was on the opposite side. Once outside (an elaborate turnstile permitted exit only), Derec breathed more freely. They were a little at a loss, this not being the way they'd come in, but the sound of the ways was obvious, and they soon found their way back to them.

"The trouble is, there's no quiet, no *private* place to talk," Ariel complained as they hesitated.

"I know. We want to go to the spaceport, but I don't feel like unfolding the map here."

"Look. . . ." Ariel fell silent until a chattering cluster of pre-teenage girls had passed, not even noticing them. "Look, the signs indicate that it isn't 'rush hour'—whatever that is—R. David mentioned it."

"Right, and lowly Fours like ourselves can ride the express platforms for many hours yet."

They made their way up the strips of the local, down again to the motionless strip between the locals and the express, then up again, faster and faster. Derec realized uneasily that if they were to trip and fall at these speeds they might be seriously injured. Nor was there an attentive robot to rush forward and grasp their arms if they should fall. Earthers never fell, he supposed. They learned when very young.

On up they went, till the wind whipped their hair and stung their eyes, up and up to the top, where each platform had a windbreak at the front of it. There they found an empty one behind a platform occupied by a man with the Mad Hatter's huge hat and sat, breathing heavily. Ariel grinned at him and Derec laughed back.

Carefully, in the shelter of the windbreak, they unfolded the map and studied it. They knew that they were in Webster Groves Section, proceeding east, and quickly found the spot, just as they passed under the sign that said SHREWS-BURY SECTION. But study the map how they would, they saw no sign of any spaceport.

Derec looked blankly at Ariel. "It's got to be here somewhere!"

A group of teenagers, mostly male, passed by two platforms away, one fleeing, the others pursuing, expertly negotiating the strips. A whistle shrilled, over the shrilling of the wind, and a blue-uniformed man waved his club and set off in pursuit of the children, who scattered down the strips. Adults scowled at them.

They studied it all over again, until the signs overhead said TOWER GROVE SECTOR.

"Possibly it isn't on the map," Ariel said. "Earthers are prejudiced against Spacers. They might not like to advertise the port."

"If you have business there, you're told how to find it, I suppose," said Derec glumly. "We should have asked R.-David how to get there."

The expressway was not straight, and as Derec looked down now, he saw that the local had spun off; another came in, made a turn, and paralleled the expressway in its place. A storefront gave way to a palatial entry that faced the oncoming expressway obliquely; above the entry was a glowing marquee on which the back view of a woman wearing tight pants appeared. She vanished, replaced by the slogan IF I WIGGLE. She reappeared, peering archly over her shoulder at the viewer: WILL YOU FOLLOW?

Derec supposed that there were as many people in view as there had been in the kitchen, and the ways were not half full, maybe not a quarter full. "Rush hour must be when the ways are full," he said.

"Yes. If they all go to work at the same time—" Ariel said, and he snapped his fingers.

"Rush, indeed." They looked about and tried to picture the swarming mobs going up and down the strips multiplied by three or four.

OLD TOWN SECTOR.

"You know," said Ariel, "Daneel Olivaw might have sat on this very platform, or at least ridden this very way."

Derec nodded. He had no memory of ever having met the famous humaniform robot, Daneel Olivaw. Daneel was designed to look exactly like a man—like Roj Nemmenuh Sarton, in fact, who had built his body. He had helped the Earthman, Plainclothesman Elijah Baley, solve the murder of Dr. Sarton, and later had gone to Solaria, where he had helped Baley solve another murder.

Han Fastolfe had built two humaniforms, the first with Sarton's help. The intricate programming that enabled a humaniform to play the part of a human being, hampered as it was by the Three Laws, was a triumph of robotics that had never been recreated. Fastolfe had refused to make more than two such robots, and one had been deactivated. Daneel Olivaw, he supposed, was still extant, somewhere on Aurora.

"Look at that hat."

Derec looked, then gaped. They had seen odd hats all along, but this woman's head was a flower garden, except that many of the "flowers" were bows. As in all Earthly hats, though, there was a prominent band for the insertion of the rating ticket that entitled them to such things as a seat during rush hour.

"You know, maybe some of these people know the way to the port," Ariel said.

That was a thought Derec had hoped she wouldn't have, but he nodded tightly. Frankly, he didn't want to speak to anyone. Perhaps because they were Earthers and he was a Spacer—with all his prejudices intact. It was a sore point with him that only Earth was exploring and settling new planets. It was not that he objected to Earth's doing that, he objected that the Spacer worlds weren't. Not these people's fault, but—

Standing up, he leaned out and got the attention of a young man—a little older than himself, he thought—who was making his way toward an unoccupied platform.

"Pardon me, sir, could you direct us to the spaceport?"

The other's rather blank expression broke into one of handsome good cheer. "Hey, gato, you do the Spacer accent ex good!" he exclaimed. "Too bad you don't have the fabric to match, but that speech'll get you on any subetheric for the asking!"

Derec concealed his confusion, lifted an eyebrow. "Yes?"

"Oh, ex, ex, that haughty look's the highest!" The other glanced around, lost his cheer, and said quietly, "But, look, this's fun and all, but I wouldn't try that speech in Yeast Town, savvy?" And with that, he was gone.

They looked at each other and shook their heads, dumb-founded.

"Do you think you could ape that—that speech of his?" Derec asked. Ariel shook her head again.

They were in a much more exalted district than Webster Groves; this Old Town Sector looked spanking new, with neat, clean, shiny buildings and prosperous-looking shops. Places of entertainment seemed more common and more lavish, as if the people who lived here had more leisure and more ration points, or money, or whichever it took, for entertainment.

"What did he mean, 'subetherics'?"

Derec thought a moment. "Hyperwave broadcasts, I think. I'm not up on that technology, but I think at one time hyperwave transmission was called that. Probably cheaper than piping cables through all these man-made caves."

Derec's voice thinned as he glanced up to where the sun should be but wasn't. Steadying his voice, he added, "I think he meant we could be entertainment stars pretending to be Spacers for Earther novels."

They grinned at each other.

EAST ST. LOUIS SECTOR.

"What does the 'ST' mean?" Neither knew.

"Derec, we're getting a long way from . . . home-kitchen. Maybe we should turn around and go back."

Derec wasn't happy about that either, but was reluctant to give up.

"Maybe one more try," he said.

He looked around for someone to ask, and was struck by the buildings in this new sector. They seemed industrial; blank fronts, a minimum of signs, a lot of which didn't even glow. All the color and gaiety seemed to have gone out of the City. Half the people on the ways had left in Old Town Sector, and no wonder.

Those who remained were far less prepossessing. They were poorly dressed and few wore hats, which meant, as Derec had gathered, that they had no passes for platform rides. Low ratings, like he and Ariel.

"What's that funny smell?" Ariel asked.

Derec sniffed, became aware of an odor. Not bread. "Something living. Maybe the ventilators don't work so good here."

"You mean we're smelling *people?*"

Derec felt a little sick himself at the thought.

"Pardon me, sir, could you direct me to the spaceport?" he asked a sullen man.

"Buzz off, gato."

Seething, Derec waited for another prospect. A woman seized a seat on a platform with such an angry, triumphant

expression that he crossed her off. Then a group of young
men and women approached, four men and two women, the
latter in gaudy, tight pants, the former all in brown corduroy.
Derec repeated his question.

The first man looked at him sharply. "Whattaya tryina
pull, gato? Spaceport! Spacer speech! Whod'ya thinkya are,
huh?"

Clamping his jaw on his anger, Derec said, "I merely
asked—"

"Oh, you merely ahsked, didja, haughty har? Whod'ya
thinkya are, I asked you, gato."

"I just wanted—"

"Clamp down, haughty har, don't go gittin' high horse
with *me*. Keep a civil tongue, and also a polite face, hear?"

Seething, Derec fought for control, and another Earther
spoke. He had a warm, dark-brown complexion and the eyes
of a hawk: racial types had remained more distinct on Earth
than on the Spacer worlds.

"Hey, Jake, I think he's rilly a Spacer. Both of 'em.
Lookit those ex fabrics."

He and Ariel were wearing plain shipsuits of synthetic
fabric, a quiet, glossy substance in different shades of gray,
hers lighter than his. Nobody had remarked on their clothes
before, but nobody had looked closely at them.

Jake stared in amazed disbelief. "Naw!"

"Yeah, Jake," one of the women shrilled, looking closely
at Ariel. "And look at 'em, both of 'em—tall and handsome, like. Spacers!"

"Spacers!" said Jake in almost reverent tones. His eyes
sharpened. "I always wanted t'meet a Spacer. Just to tell 'em
what I think of 'em!"

"Yeah!"

"You think you're so smart, doin' your little social
science investigation of 'Earther' society, huh, Spacer?"
This time it sounded like a spit.

Derec's anger cooled in apprehension; Ariel had unobtru-
sively taken his arm. "Thanks for your help, but we've got
to be going."

Again his accent aroused their ire.

They all began to jabber hostilely as he and Ariel stepped to one side, were struck by the wind, and fell behind on their slower strip.

"Stop! We ain't done talkin' atya!" cried Jake, and the Earthers swarmed off the platform level and started down.

Ariel gasped and Derec realized that they would soon be below them, on the slower strips, between them and the locals.

"Back up!" Derec said tensely, and in a moment they were squeezing between platforms. Their persecutors caught the change of direction instantly and were in full cry.

He hurried Ariel rapidly down the strips on the inside, their enemies gaining rapidly with a lifetime's expertise. At the motionless median between expressways, he looked around wildly. There was no possibility of their climbing the reverse ways and staying ahead.

"In here!" said Ariel, and they dived into a kiosk and ran down the strip, not waiting for it to carry them. They ran under the ways, hearing voices crying "Spacer! Spacer!" behind them.

At the other end, they had a choice of a moving strip that would take them up beside the expressway, or a maze of corridors at this level: poorly lit, poorly cleaned, sparsely populated, and thick with nameless organic odors.

There was quite a mob behind them, by the sound. Panting, they ran into the first corridor, took the first branching, then the next. They paused, listening. A derelict lay on a low platform beside a wide freight door, scruffy and unshaven. ST. LOUIS YEAST, PLANT 17, said the door.

Derec had a sudden flashing memory of having viewed a novel set on Earth in the medieval days, when a derelict like this turned out to be a crusty, cheerful, picaresque, heart-of-gold character who saved the day for the hero and became his closest buddy.

This one had more the attitude of a rat. Rousing himself with surprising energy, he listened, rubbed his graying whiskers, and, growling something about "stirring up the damn yeast farmers," he dived into a small door beside the freight door, and slammed it. They heard it lock.

Voices and footfalls approached. They looked around. There were no tiny crannies to escape into, nothing but corridors wide enough for trucks to be driven through. Eventually they'd be run down wherever they went, however fast they ran. And their enemies no longer merely wanted to talk to Derec and Ariel. They had something much more direct in mind.

CHAPTER 5
ESCAPE?

Ariel heard them coming. Heart pounding, she looked around again. No place to run to, no place to hide. After a blank moment Derec took the Key to Perihelion out of his pocket (Ariel gasped), put it in her palm, squeezed the four corners in succession, and closed both their hands around it fiercely. Ariel pushed the button as they held their breath.

The gray nothingness of Perihelion was around them, forever and ever to the limits of vision.

Derec let his breath out. "Frost! I thought they had us!"

"So did I!"

They were in no hurry to return to Earth, yet there was surely no more boring place in hyperspace or normal space, whichever it was, than Perihelion. They looked at each other, and Ariel shrugged, as Derec wiped his brow.

"Oh, no!"

They had moved at the same time, and, releasing each other, had drifted apart. With great presence of mind, Derec lunged for her. Ariel was frozen in shock; had she reached for him at the same time, she could have caught his hand. Too late.

They looked at each other tragically. Inexorably, they drifted further apart.

Ariel felt she had to make up for it. "I'll throw you the Key!" she cried. "You go back to Earth—forget about me!"

"Nonsense! If you do, I'll throw it back—"

At that moment his face went blank and he contorted himself into a knot; reaching for his soft shoes, he tore them off. Writhing with a practiced free-fall motion, he turned his back to her and hurled the first shoe away. With the reaction to that throw, he ceased to recede. Now he was rotating. He allowed himself to rotate twice, studying her, then writhed again, and threw the other shoe.

After a prolonged wait they seized each other, Ariel gasping in relief. To her surprise, she felt him shaking.

"Derec, you were marvelous! I thought we were lost!"

Derec grinned shakily. "What you said about throwing the Key gave me the idea."

"Frost, I'm glad something did." Ariel took the Key and pressed the corners again, and, with both gripping it, pushed the button.

R. David was against the wall in his usual place.

"Frost," Ariel said, feeling ready to collapse. She sat down, knees shaking, and so did Derec.

"What did they mean, 'your little social study of conditions on Earth'—the yeast farmers?" Derec asked.

Ariel had no idea. They put the question to R. David, careful not to let him know that they had been in serious danger.

He said, "I have no access to news feed, but I believe that Dr. Avery made some public announcement about studying social conditions on Earth when he first contacted Earthly authorities to transfer rare metals for money. He promised not to send in humaniform robots, and of course it did not occur to the authorities that he would enter Earthly society himself."

"Then how did he expect to make any study of Earth society?" Ariel asked, skeptical.

"He purchased many Earthly studies of the subject, and also me. While ostensibly studying these sources, he quietly developed the medical prophylaxis with which I treated you, and infiltrated Earth society in his own person, learning what kinds of identification and ration media he would need to have to pretend to be an Earthman. Some of those he bought openly as samples for his study. In short, over a period of an Earthly year he was occasionally in the news as he came and went from Earth. And from this study he was allegedly making, I suppose that rumors may have gone abroad that teams of Spacers are studying Earthly sociology on the spot. That is, of course, very unlikely."

"Very," said Derec, with a grimace. "Spacers are just not interested in the subject, and if they were, they wouldn't take the health risk."

Ariel could not care less about Earth's rumors. "The important thing is to get back into space," she said.

"You're right," Derec said. "I'm more than tired of concrete caves and the troglodytes that live in them." She smiled fleetingly at the term. "So the third thing is to find out how to get to the spaceport. The first being to have those directions to the nearest Personal repeated, and the second, to find a shoe store."

Ariel grimaced, but said, "You're right."

When put to the question, R. David said, "The spaceport is located near New York, Miss Avery."

They looked at each other blankly. Of course they knew that there were eight hundred Cities on Earth. They had been thinking in terms of one giant City covering all Earth, the natural extension of their Earthly experience.

"What City is this, then?" Ariel asked.

"The City of Saint Louis," said R. David. "It is on the same continent as New York, so travel is facilitated. One may take the train, and for a third of the distance the way is enclosed and roofed over. It takes less than twelve hours— half an Earthly rotation, Mr. Avery." He had detected the question on Derec's face.

Ariel had no idea what a "train" might be, and wasn't happy about its being enclosed—she visualized something like the expressway. She looked at Derec, who looked equally unhappy.

"Do we have the money—the rating or whatever—to go on the train?" Derec asked dubiously.

R. David said, "Your travel vouchers have not been touched, but I believe there is an inadequate amount. As

Fours, you do not rate much, nor do many Earth people often travel between Cities."

"Even though we are Transients?"

"You are Transients in this sector, but not necessarily in this City."

"We'd better visit the Personal first," said Ariel tiredly. "We'll think it over when we get back."

R. David repeated his directions to the Personals, which turned out to be in opposite directions. Rather reluctantly, they split up, and Derec left with a backward glance. Ariel walked slowly toward the women's Personal, hoping Derec's stockinged feet would not be too noticeable.

Since this was the Personal assigned to her, Ariel found a shower cubby with the same number as the one on her tag, and took a shower. Again, no towels; she saw a woman carrying a little cloth satchel into a similar cubby and presumed it contained a towel, combs, and so on. She wouldn't need one, as short a time as they expected to be on Earth. She had, of course, brought a comb, though she should see about getting a brush. Fortunately, her hair wasn't long.

She made her way back to Sub-Section G, Corridor M, Sub-Corridor 16, Apartment 21, without difficulty, hardly seeing the crowds of Earthers who swarmed through the passageways.

Derec was back before her and full of energy. Despite their brush with the mob, he wanted to go check out the "train station." He was careful not to say so in front of R. David, who might think it dangerous, but she thought he wanted to see if they could devise a method of stowing away.

Showing them on the map, R. David gave them directions that would take them, by the route they had previously followed, to Old Town and something called the Gateway Arch Plaza. The station was beneath that. They would pass several shoe stores on the way.

Ariel felt distinctly nervous as they threaded their way again through the corridors to the junction and took the down ramp, but nobody paid any attention to them. She would have liked to have changed clothes, but their shipsuits were all they had, and they weren't all that conspicuous. It still wasn't rush hour, so they had the freedom of the express platforms, and went straight up to them on the eastbound side.

The clerk in the shoe store was a human, a plump, youngish woman, older than Ariel. She quirked her mouth in a half-humorous fashion at Derec's socks and said, "Been running the strips, eh?" She produced neat, cheap shoes expeditiously, checked his ration tag in her machine, accepted the money tag, and waved them away, calling, "Next time be more careful of the edges!"

Back to the expressway.

She heard Derec's breath speed up beside her, as Old Town Sector came rushing toward them, but they saw none of the yeast farmers from before—less than an hour ago.

"I'll walk the rest of the way before I'll ride this thing into—Yeast Town," she said, leaning over to shout at Derec.

"Yeah," he said weakly. Ariel saw that he was staring up at the high ceiling, which was higher here than in Webster Groves. There was probably nothing overhead but the roof of the City, for here the ways were in a great slash through the building blocks. No matter—he was having a claustrophobic attack.

Ariel sympathized—she had had several of them herself. At the moment it was the crowds, not the oppressive buildings, that made her own breath come short.

Before she could attempt to reassure him, Derec gripped her arm and pointed: *Gateway-Arch Plaza Exit*. They descended hastily and rode the ramp down under the ways, found a sign pointing north, and followed it to a localway, also plainly marked.

Presently they entered the Gateway-Arch Plaza.

It was enormous. Gaping like rubes, they stepped out of the way of swarms of chattering Earthers, and frankly stared. The Gateway Arch itself was smaller, perhaps, than the Pillar of the Dawn on Aurora that commemorated the early pioneers, and surely was less moving than the memorial at the pillar's base, where outstanding men and women of each generation were honored. But at a hundred ninety meters tall, the arch was no small monument. Its span was nearly equal to its height, and the roof was another ten meters above it. It was all matte stainless steel, ancient looking but in good repair.

The room that enclosed the whole mastodonic fabrication was commensurate in size, over two hundred meters in diameter, its circular walls a cliff of concrete and metal around the arch. This cliff was covered with the balconies of high-rated apartments.

Derec walked boldly toward the lower area between the feet of the arch, and Ariel followed, inwardly amused at the awe on the faces of some of the Earthmen—some showed unmistakable signs of agoraphobia, exposed to this much open space.

Below the arch was a museum dating from pre-space-flight times, which might have been interesting, but they were looking for a train station. Quietly determined to ask no directions, they wasted half an hour, some of it in looking at exhibits. Ariel was struck by the unfinished look of the items people used in the pre-industrial age, all made by crude hand methods. Derec pointed out a plaque that stated that, in the old days, citizens had ridden a sort of tramway up inside the arch.

"Agoraphobia," he said, echoing her thought.

Ariel nodded and led him briskly out of the museum. It felt like underground to her, and the crowds of Earthers swarming around were bringing on another claustrophobic attack. She felt much more sympathetic to them and less inclined to sneer at Earthly phobias.

They had to leave the plaza itself to find the route to the station; they had been following the plaza signs and hadn't noticed the station signs when they left the localway. The staion was a level or two deeper, and a different route took them there.

There were fewer people here, but below the passenger

level they found a series of freightways crisscrossing the
City, which carried heavy items in bulk containers. Many
men in rough clothing rode these ways in handling carts,
shunting the big containers off the belts at their destinations.
These freightways all traveled at a walking pace, no more.

At the station they also found the terminus of a tube system for small capsules. Letters and small items—parcel
post—could be blown about the City very rapidly by this
system, and Derec became quite excited by it.

He'd seen a system like this before, on a somewhat different scale. The Robot City robots had generated a tremendous vacuum as a side effect of their Key-manufacturing
facility, and Derec and Ariel had ridden the vacuum tubes
more than once when they were in a hurry.

But here on Earth they were using the same technology
not because they had a vacuum they could use; they had to
create a vacuum to make it work. In one form or another,
Derec knew, vacuum tubes like these had been used since
the early industrial age—and Earth had apparently never
discarded their use, because on Earth they made sense.

"Much more efficient than sending a car with a robot," he
said.

It is if your houses are close together, Ariel thought. On
the Spacer worlds, they were scattered.

The station seemed to deal mostly in inter-urban freight,
but there was a window for passenger traffic. They avoided
it, and prowled along the cars.

The train was no moving beltway, as Ariel had expected.
Derec was clearly disappointed; he had expected something
like the expressway. These were cars with ridiculously tiny
wheels, and after a while Derec decided that they used magnetic levitation under speed. It was a very old technique.

"Now I see what R. David meant by saying that the way
is largely roofed over," Ariel said.

"Twelve hours in one of those, eh?" Derec said, bleakly.

The cars had no windows.

"Hey! Hey, you! You kids!"

They turned, concealing their apprehension.

A rough-looking stranger approached, wearing blue canvas and a peaked cap with stripes of pale gray and darker blue-gray, very distinctive. CONTINENTAL RAILROAD, said the emblem on his chest.

"What are you doing here?"

"Looking at the train, sir," said Derec, after a moment, trying to mimic the Earth dialect.

The other did not notice that. He closed in and examined them sharply, a beefy individual, taller than either of them and looking as if he worked out every day.

"Why?" he asked, irritably.

"School assignment, sir," said Ariel, thinking quickly.

He looked at her sharply again in her tight shipsuit, and she realized with a despairing feeling that she no longer had the figure of a schoolgirl. But he nodded, more in appreciation of her than in agreement, and said, more reasonably, "A study of the Continental system, eh? Well, you'll not learn much by prowling the yards. Read your books. But I can show you the marshaling yard and the loading docks. You should've brought visual recorders."

Evidently their new acquaintance—Peter, or Dieter, Scanlan—had little to do at the moment and was bored. Taking them briskly back the way they had come, he showed them where the cars were pulled aside, their doors opened, and men in handling machines carried forth containers of assorted cargo.

"That lot is bulk cargo, mostly—wheat from Kansas and points north," Scanlan shouted over the constant rumble of wheels and the whine of electric motors. "Now, over there —see those big blue cars?—that's pigs of metals from the seawater refineries on the Gulf, down south-away. You'll see some manufactured goods going out, and quite a bit coming in—St. Louis mostly exports food, especially gourmet items. Not a big manufacturing city like Detroit."

What Ariel saw was that each of these big cars was crammed full of containers cunningly stacked to fill every corner, leaving no wasted space for even a rat to hide in.

"Come this way," said Scanlan, and he put them on a tiny truck like a motorized platform.

Its control was purely manual and Ariel fought down fear as she joined the men on it. Scanlan sent it hurtling around the fringes of activity to dive into a bright tunnel, which branched, branched again, and minutes later and two kilometers away he braked to a halt at a balcony.

They looked down on the marshaling yards.

"Trains are made up here," he shouted—it was noisy here, too.

Ariel looked, and realized why they were called "trains": each was a long series of units like link sausages. The cars were the units. They were being driven individually along the floor to the marked "rails" or roads painted on the floor, to the trains they were to make up. Each train was made up in a specific order.

"Over there to your left—passenger train for the West Coast. Three cars in blue, with silver and gold trim."

It was crawling slowly on its wheels toward, she supposed, the ticket window and embarking ramp. Once in the tunnels the cars would be lifted off their wheels by the magnetic rails.

On their right was a train of a hundred cars, in various colors according to what cargo they carried. That seemed to be the ratio of passengers to freight, except that there were more freight trains than passenger trains.

"Computer-controlled," shouted Scanlan. "There's a driver in each car for safety, but the computer does most of the placing. It knows where each car goes in the train. They pick up new cars at each stop on the front end, and drop off cars from the tail. The computer also knows which container is in each car, and what's in each container.

"Down here!"

Scanlan started the vehicle up again, whirled them down and down, braked in a flood of light. Black water lapped ahead of them, boats bobbing on it under the low ceiling.

"The Mississippi," he said, hissing like a snake. "Trans-shipment docks!"

They'd seen enough, but had to submit to another half-hour of education on a subject they could not—now—care less about.

They weren't going to be using the train.

CHAPTER 6
STUDIES IN SOCIOLOGY

Derec sighed with relief when they reentered the cheerless little apartment.

"I'm—tired," said Ariel. "I need to rest."

"Sure, you go lie down," said Derec, instantly concerned and quite understanding. He was exhausted and disappointed also. It had been a long day.

R. David stepped forward and unnecessarily showed her how to work the dimmer in the bedroom. It felt good to be back where robotic concern, the basis of all truly civilized societies, was available.

Derec sat down, thinking of that, and felt vaguely dissatisfied. He had always taken that statement for granted, and considered Earth uncivilized, in the lofty Spacer manner. *No wonder,* he thought slowly, *that Spacers are resented on Earth.* Because those people seemed to get along quite well without robots. That commissary might seem like an animal feeding trough to the overrefined sensibilities of a Spacer, but was that just? Human beings could adapt to a wide variety of societies. If Earthers were adapted to a way of life that gave Spacers the heebie-jeebies, it did not necessarily follow that Earth society was inferior.

True, Earth's Cities were the end product of an artificial process, and were highly unstable. If power supplies were interrupted for an hour, every human in the City would die of asphyxiation. Water was nearly as critical, and food almost as critical as water. Nor could the people leave the

Cities in case of emergency; there was no place to go, and in any case, they could not bear the open air.

That train system could not begin to evacuate them, assuming it had power when the City didn't.

Was not Spacer society, though, with its dependence on robots, in its way just as artificial and dependent as Earth's? It was a novel and alarming thought. True, the robots could not all be simultaneously stricken by some plague, nor would all the factories shut down and not be reopened before the last robot wore out. They were not going to be deprived of their robots and robotic care.

No, Derec thought uneasily, *it was a more serious problem than that.* More serious even than Spacers' reliance on robots to save them from their own folly. Derec had had all he could do to keep from stopping and looking back to watch their pursuers being seized by the robots he knew *must* be there. Beyond that reliance, which was actually quite trivial, was the freezing of their whole society.

When a robot was unable to respond, caught between conflicting demands of the Laws of Robotics, it was said to be in "mental freeze-out." All of Spacer society, he suspected, might be in mental freeze-out, or at least in stasis. It was the Earthers, after all, who were settling the galaxy.

Somberly, he thought: *The only solution might be to give up robots. Or at least restrict their numbers.*

In the meantime, Dr. Avery had some mad scheme for spreading advanced robots all across a planet, and then, apparently, peopling it with humans.

With that thought in his mind, Derec drifted off to sleep, and was not conscious of R. David springing forward to keep him from falling off the couch.

Derec dreamed.

He had swollen to enormous size, and larger, and larger. He was a planet, and something was crawling across his stomach. Raising his head and peering at the swollen dome of his belly, he saw that it was a city. Not an Earthly City, but a city of buildings separated by streets. A city populated by robots, ever-changing as buildings were built, torn down, rebuilt in different shapes. It was Robot City, and it spread around his equator.

He watched in fascination for a time, in fascination and horror—this was wrong, wrong, it was a spreading disease —and then he heard Ariel's voice.

No! The Human Medical Team was carrying her lifeless body sadly toward the crematorium. He struggled to move, to cry out . . . but he no longer had hands, or a voice—

Ariel was shaking him awake; he lay in a cramped position on the couch. R. David hovered in concern behind her.

"You were sleeping peacefully, then started struggling when you heard my voice. Sorry."

"Nothing," he managed. "Just a nightmare."

"Ah." She turned to R. David and began to question him while Derec sat on the couch, arms dangling, still badly shaken by the nightmare, telling himself it was only a dream. Only a dream.

But it gripped him, shook him as badly as the pursuit by the yeast farmers had done. He threw it off and looked up as Ariel turned to him.

"I've been asking about news," she said in a complaining tone. "There's no broadcast reception in this apartment, not of any kind. Frost! No news, no entertainment—there's only the book-viewer. Not even an audio for music!"

"This apartment is for solitary Step Threes of various ratings," said R. David soothingly. "Step Threes are expected to consume their entertainment at the public facilities."

"It's probably for youngsters with low-paying entry-level jobs, just getting away from their parents," Derec said vaguely.

He looked closely at Ariel. During their excursions on the expressway she had seemed alive, vital, healthy. Now she seemed tired, petulant, lethargic. Fear gripped his heart like a fist.

"I'm tired of being cooped up. I want out!" she said.

Derec had to slow his own breathing and wait till his heart stopped pounding. "So do I," he said, his tone so controlled that despite her lethargy she glanced quickly at him.

R. David's face was not made to express his concern. "Few Earth people leave their Cities, but there are some with a perverse attraction for openness and isolation. These direct the robots of the mines and farms, and man certain industrial facilities distant from the Cities for safety reasons. Other Earthers, wishing to become Settlers, join conditioning schools that accustom them to space and openness."

"Settlers!" said Ariel with surprise.

"Of course," said Derec wonderingly. "We know Earth people never leave their Cities; we also know that they alone are settling new planets. We should have made the connection long since. Conditioning is the only answer."

"Could we join one of these schools?" she asked.

"It would take us outdoors," said Derec uncertainly. But as he thought about it he shook his head. "I suspect that applicants for Settler worlds are investigated pretty strictly."

"Oh. Then—the other?"

Derec didn't know. "If we could get a job on a farm, directing robots . . ." He turned to R. David. "How are these workers chosen?"

"I am not sure of the details, but I suppose that one must apply for the job," said R. David.

Something Scanlan had said occurred to Derec. "Food and other raw materials are brought in from the surrounding areas by truck," he said. "Maybe, if we got jobs driving trucks—"

He didn't care to finish the sentence, not knowing to what extent R. David would condone violations of Earth laws. Ariel caught his meaning at once however and her eyes brightened.

How long it would take to drive a distance that a train could travel in twelve hours, he didn't know. What kind of pursuit they could expect, he had no idea. But nothing else seemed even remotely feasible.

R. David told them how to find out what they needed to know: the nearest communo would give them most of the information they needed for a start. Ariel's mood had lifted again, and again they ventured forth.

They consulted the directory at the communo, found Job Service, and checked *Farms—truck drivers*. A number of company names were listed, and Derec chose the Missouri Farm Company at random. It immediately transmitted an application form for them, which they could fill out by answering verbally when the pointer moved from question to question.

The first question was, *Do you have a driver's license?*

Derec sighed and canceled everything, went back to the menu, and did some exploring.

"I wish there was an information robot we could call up and ask," he said, frustrated.

It turned out that many Earthers who never went outside the City needed to know how to drive. There were schools, which taught them according to the regulations—and the instructions and regulations, being government-standardized, were readily available. They only had to take a book card and go to a library, then pay to have them printed off.

Another request gave them a map of the area, with YOU ARE HERE labeled and TARGET: *Library* indicated. They compared that to their own map, and nodded.

Opening the door of the communo booth made it switch back from opaque to clear, and they were given a sour look by the middle-aged fellow waiting for it.

"Canntchee find a private place out of people's way?" he growled, lurching past them.

Derec turned red, half with anger, half with embarrassment. Ariel was equally angry and much less embarrassed.

They walked away, seething, and observed that the playground was largely deserted. It was getting late.

"I hope we're not too late," he said.

"Yes." After a moment, Ariel said, "I suppose Earthers have a lot of trouble courting."

She had a point. No pleasant, nearly empty gardens for them to walk in on fine days; no large rambling mansions to prowl through on wet ones. What did they do? Derec wondered what he and Ariel might have done, back in his unremembered past.

It had been the leading edge of the rush hour when they had arrived back home from the train station. Now all that was over, and the people were leaving the section kitchen in droves. They had only eaten twice today, both times fairly early—and neither had eaten much on the ship.

"Frost, they're still open," said Derec. "I thought we'd go hungry all night."

"So did I," said Ariel.

The line moved rapidly and they were soon in, and were astonished to find that free choice had not been suspended. They were assigned to table F-3 this time. The place, with only a couple of thousand people in it, seemed deserted.

The table, when they found it, had probably been used by three or four relays of diners for the evening meal, but it was surprisingly clean and neat. They saw Earthers industriously wiping up their places prior to leaving. Others, attendants, came around with cleansing utensils that seemed almost superfluous; some sprayed the places with steam guns to sterilize them.

They were far enough from their neighbors to speak freely in low tones. "I suppose there are strong social forces to make them clean up their places," Ariel said.

Derec thought about it, nodded. Mere laws could not have such force. "I suppose they train their kids: Clean up your places. What'll the neighbors think?"

"The forces for conformity to social norms must be tremendous," she said. "It's not necessarily a bad thing."

"It makes their whole civilization possible. And are we that different?" he asked.

Ariel shook her head somberly. She had been exiled for violating some of those norms.

They were given three choices: Zymosteak, again, Sweet-and-Pungent Zymopork, and Pseudo-Chicken Casserole. Side dishes included such things as salads and fruit plates, Hearty Hungarian Goulash, Vegetable Pseudo-Beef

Stew, and so on. They chose the Zymopork and the Casserole, and browsed among the side dishes, almost famishing from the smell of the food around them.

"At least, seated here in the middle, we can watch the families," Ariel said.

"Right. I was wondering if it would be acceptable to divide our dishes with each other. But see that family with the four kids—the kids are swapping around ad lib."

"Yes—and the parents. Different side dishes come with different main courses, and they're trading off."

The food arrived at that point, and they wasted no more time watching others eat.

When they had finished and exited the kitchen, Derec paused, glancing around.

"What's wrong?"

"It's still light," he said. "It should be getting dark."

She laughed nervously. They moved aside, out of the way, and strolled slowly toward the ways. "I know what you mean. Especially for us, since we got up well before what these people consider the dawn. But, of course, the lights will never dim."

They rode the localway for a short distance, changed ways, and presently found themselves at a massive entrance flanked with stone lions.

"Stone!" said Ariel, sounding astonished. "I supposed they'd be plastic or something."

"Or nothing," said Derec. He liked libraries, though people rarely visited them on the Spacer worlds. It was simpler just to call them up and have the books transmitted over your phone.

"I suppose many apartments on Earth must be equipped to receive book transmissions," he said.

"In higher social classes," Ariel said wryly, and he laughed. Spacers though they were, they were not masquerading merely as Earthers, but as low-rated Earthers.

Crowds of people, as usual on Earth, swarmed up and down the ornamental steps that led up to the entry. Some sat on the steps or the balusters, talking, laughing, eating or drinking, and many reading. A group of children played on one of the lions, their book-viewers laid carefully between its paws. Inside were uniformed guards with clubs and surprisingly cheerful expressions, sober people of all ages swarming about, many of them young, and people sitting around tables. Virtually every terminal was in use.

"This must be the library's rush hour," Derec whispered.

With school out for the day, people off work and looking for the cheapest entertainment—it probably was.

At length they found an unused terminal and did a twenty-minute search for the information, making sure they had all they needed. Derec had a moment of doubt when he inserted his money tab into the slot. This metal tab was not unlike the credit-transfer system on the Spacer worlds. But he had no idea what formalities were employed here, or how much money there was in this account.

ACCEPTED, said the blinking transparency, and the machine tinkled a tune to let them know it was copying the information on their card.

"We've got it," he said, breathing more easily. "Let's go."

Out of the library, down the steps, to the right. They marched more slowly than they had at the beginning of the day. Derec was as tired as Ariel looked.

"It's been a *long* day," he said hollowly.

"And we've come a long way," she added.

Turn, and turn again, and they confronted a smaller marquee than one they'd seen in Old Town Sector: WILL YOU FOLLOW?

"Not tonight, honey," said Derec vaguely. "I'm too tired."

"We didn't come by that, Derec," Ariel said, gripping his arm.

"I know," he said tiredly. "We've gotten turned around."

They retraced their steps, and now couldn't find the library. After quite a while they paused, gray-faced with weariness and strain, before a window showing dresses and hats of incredible fabrics, some of which glowed. Cheap finery.

Men and women peered through windows, pointed out things they'd like but would probably never afford. Not far from them a young man in tight blue pants and silver pseudo-leather jacket, with elaborately coiffed hair, stood next to a girl who seemed much older than Ariel and who wore even tighter violet pants and a nearly transparent, slashed top. Her hair was blonde and long on one side and short and red on the other, and her eyes were cynical and hard.

This was a major thoroughfare, though it was not part of the moving way system. It ought to join to the ways somewhere, but didn't seem to. They had no idea which way to go.

"Just like a couple of Transients," said Derec glumly. "We can't be far from the ways, but we could spend an hour blundering around looking for them."

The youth with the tough expression and the silvery jacket turned toward them.

"Transients, eh?" he said. He looked them up and down. The hard-featured young woman looked at them curiously also.

Derec braced himself.

CHAPTER 7
BACK TO SCHOOL

"That way two blocks, take the up ramp," the young tough said courteously, and the hard-featured young woman looked sympathetically at them.

"Thank you," said Derec, and Ariel, as startled as he, echoed him.

Their rescuers had forgotten them before they were out of sight, but Derec and Ariel remembered them all the way home.

The section kitchen had become a familiar place by the time of their third meal, next morning. Much of the shock of enormous rooms, enormous numbers of loud talking Earthers, of being ignored amid mobs, was gone. After breakfast, out into the monotonous every-day of the ways, they rode south toward the edge of the sprawling megalopolis. Finally, in a section called Mattese, they found the driving school they sought.

They had chosen it because it was a "private" school. Though regulated by the government, it counted as a luxury, and one paid for the privilege of learning here, a concept that bemused the Spacers.

"Yes, please?"

The receptionist was not the robot the term called to their minds, but a middle-aged woman—though Earthers aged fast by Spacer standards; she was probably quite young, perhaps no more than forty-five or fifty.

"Derec and Ariel Avery," Derec said apologetically, trying again to imitate the Earth dialect.

"Oh, yes, new students. You're a bit early, but that's good—you have to do your forms."

They thought they'd already done the forms over the communo, but took the papers and sat down. These forms were simple and asked primarily how much experience they'd had with automobiles and something called "models."

"Can that mean whàt I think it does?" Ariel asked. Derec could only shrug.

They had sweated over the application last night, for it asked for their schooling, but R. David had given them the names of schools in the City they might have gone to. They hoped the driving school would be lax in checking up. Of course, sooner or later their imposture would be detected, but even one day, they calculated—

"You may see Ms. Winters now," said the receptionist, smiling kindly.

Ms. Winters kept them waiting in an outer office for a moment while she examined their forms, and Ariel nudged Derec.

"Did you hear that receptionist? She was trying to copy *our* accent!"

Ms. Winters called them in, asked a question or two, nodded, and, taking the forms, left with a brief "Wait just a moment." It hadn't taken her long, as they had indicated no experience.

She hadn't closed the door completely.

"Red? Those two students, the brother and sister . . . upper-rating children slumming, or kicked out of the house, or something." Doubtfully, she added, "Maybe student reporters, checking up on the schooling system, or something."

"Who cares?" came a gruff-sounding male voice. "They got money, they want to learn, we sell schoolin'. Send 'em on out."

With a dazzling smile, Ms. Winters ushered them through the farther door into a large room with a number of carrels within it. Students were entering in a steady stream from a different door and occupying carrels and other learning stations farther down.

Red confronted them, a blocky fellow with thinning sandy hair and a handsome face, his body one solid slab of muscle. He looked them over shrewdly for a moment, nodded, gave a noncommittal grunt.

"Drivin's a hands-on schoolin'," he said bluntly. "You either learn it with your reflexes or else you don't learn it. It ain't so different from learnin' to ride the ways, though you don't remember how you did that." It was a set speech, and went on in that vein for about three minutes. Red's face remained blank.

Derec was impressed despite his prejudices. Education among Spacers, as little of it as he could remember, was a more gracious process, lavishly supported by ever-patient robots. It was clear that this indifferent man proposed to push them into the water and watch to see if they drowned. If they did not, they would be rewarded only by his good opinion.

". . . it's your money and your time, so I know you'll do your best and not waste either."

Though his experience with different machines must be far greater than this Earther's, Derec wryly found that Red's good opinion was a thing worth striving for.

The carrels were cockpits containing mockups of the control sets of various kinds of vehicles, and trimensionals of the roadways. Red gave them a brief instruction on the rules of the road and the operation of the craft, showed them a printed set of instructions on the right and of rules on the left, and said, "Do it, gatos."

Derec and Ariel grinned faintly at each other, and *did it* for about half an hour.

Red came by at the end of the time, sucking on the stem of a cup, if a cup had a stem, and exhaling smoke courteously away from them. He bent and looked on the back sides of the carrels.

"You did good," he said, his eyebrows expressing more than his voice. "You did real good, for beginners."

Maybe too good, Derec thought uneasily.

Red looked at them, blew smoke thoughtfully, and said, "Come down here to the models."

The models were as they had supposed, small-scale versions of various vehicles they'd have to learn to drive in order to graduate, from one-man scooters to big transport trucks. They were given models of four-person passenger cars marked POLICE, and control sets, the models being, of course, remote-controlled.

This was an interactive game with a vengeance, and the other students who had advanced this far grinned at them and made room. Derec started his car slowly, nearly got run over by a big truck, speeded up, nearly went out of the lane going around a corner, cut too sharply, but gradually began to get the hang of it.

Then a white-gleaming ambulance with red crosses on its doors and top made a left turn from the outside lane, the operator crying "Oops!" belatedly as he realized where he was. Derec avoided him skillfully and slipped past. After a moment his controls froze, as did the ambulance's. The ambulance operator grimaced, then grinned ruefully, and they all looked at a trimensional screen to one side.

A-9 ILLEGAL TURN, NO SIGNALS. P-3, FAILURE TO APPREHEND TRAFFIC VIOLATOR.

"Frost. Swim or drown," Derec muttered, and the girl next to him laughed.

It wasn't as easy as it looked, and he wasn't *thinking* only of not knowing the rules—such as that a police car was expected to act like a police car. The streets were full of vehicles, and he had to be prepared to predict their moves. None of his Spacer training was of much use here. To his mortification, he rammed a fire engine at one stopping, not seeing the signal lights in time. It didn't help that Ariel slaughtered half a dozen pedestrians at a place where the motorway and pedestrian levels merged. The other students were far better, but cheerful about it, or Derec couldn't have stood it.

It was humiliating.

After an hour of exhilarating play, during which they got much better, Red came by and said, "Take a break, all; give the second team a chance."

The students relinquished their controls, leaving the vehicles in mid-street, and trooped out, old and young alike, to some kind of refectory. Red caught Derec's eye, nodded to Ariel; they stepped aside.

"I've been watching the monitor record. You're not so swift on models, where I was expectin' you t' shine," he said. "Figured you'd have lots of experience on them."

He paused and eyed them questioningly, but they just nodded. Shrugging, Red said, "I'm gonna put you on trucks. Big ones. You ever been outside?"

Chilled, Derec said, "What?"

"Outside the City," Red said patiently.

"Well—" Derec exchanged a glance with Ariel. "Yeah. We've, uh, we've given it a try."

"Ever have nightmares about it?"

"What? No."

Red nodded shrewdly. "The shrinks have all kinds tests, but one thing talks true: nightmares. Thing is, you're young, you could be conditioned easily if you aren't what shrinks call phobic. That means, if you don't have nightmares. Big money in driving the big rigs outside—not many people to do this kind of job. Most trucks are computer-controlled, or remote-controlled—but even remote-control ops get upset, break down, have nightmares. They even use a lot of robot drivers."

"Really?"

Red shrugged. "Why not? They're not takin' anybody's job away. Not many people will do that kind of work. If you can do it—and will—it pays real good."

Derec and Ariel looked at each other.

"Don't have to decide right away," Red said shrewdly. "I know—people'd think you're queer, wanting to go outside. And I should tell you, I get a bounty on every prospect I send out."

He looked at them with a hint of humor. "Oh, yeah, you

got to apply for the job—outside."

He paused for an answer, and Derec said slowly, "Well, can we think it over? I mean, we don't know anything about trucks—"

"I'll put you on simulators now—c'mon back here."

At the back of the room were giant simulators they had to climb up into—three of them.

"Most of the trucks we train on are for inside the City, and they're pretty small. Lots of competition for the driver jobs on them—most freight goes by the freightways, naturally, and driving the freight-handler trucks is a different department of the Transportation Bureau. Lots of competition for those jobs, too. But these big babies go beggin'. Yet they're real easy to learn."

The important thing was remembering that one had a long "tail" behind one. They moved slowly when maneuvering, though, and anyone who had landed a spaceship could learn this readily enough.

"Give it half an hour or so, an' we'll look at your records."

It was closer to an hour, and Derec and Ariel were both tired when Red approached them again.

"You done real good," he said, looking at a print-out. "You were made for outside drivin'. You do much better where you don't have to watch out for traffic." He looked at them with a faint smile. "It's never as frantic in the motorways as in our model. Usually they're wide open and empty. But you learn about traffic *in* traffic."

"How'd we do?" Ariel asked, imitating his accent fairly well, to Derec's ear.

"Good enough to make it worth your while to go on," said Red. "A week's training, and I'll be sending you out to Mattell Trucking & Transport. Yes?"

Ms. Winters, from the inner office, had approached him. She glanced at them curiously.

"You two go take a break, drink some fruit juice or something, and I'll talk to you in fifteen minutes."

When they were out of sight, Ariel said, "Keep on going."

"I thought so, but I couldn't be sure," Derec said.

"I suppose she checked out our education, or something," Ariel said glumly.

"Yes, well, it had to happen. And we've had an hour's worth of training on big trucks." Derec was quite buoyant. "I doubt very much if they are equipped to chase stolen trucks across the countryside. At least, not well equipped. How many Earthers would not only steal a big truck, but take off across country?"

"We haven't stolen our truck yet," Ariel said gloomily.

Derec found himself joining her in gloom as they made their way back to the expressway; and then they found it jammed and had to stand on the lower-ratings' level. It traveled just as fast, but it was a tiring nuisance.

They stopped off at the kitchen for a light lunch, and at the Personals on the way back to the apartment. Derec made his way back to Sub-Section G, Corridor M, Sub-Corridor 16, Apartment 21, from the Personal, with a skill that was by now automatic. Then he sat and waited. And waited.

Derec was quite concerned by the time Ariel returned, and became more concerned with one look at her. She had taken twice as long as he, and looked dull.

"What took you so long?"

"I got lost," she said lusterlessly.

"You look—tired. You want—to lie down?" Derec's voice kept catching with his fear.

"I guess."

But Ariel sat down on the couch and didn't move. She didn't respond to anything Derec said. After a long while she got up and dragged herself into the bedroom.

Derec was worried and restless. He had wanted to discuss ways and means of getting a truck, but that was impossible under the circumstances. She obviously had at least a mild fever.

Instead, he spent the afternoon viewing books. Some of

Dr. Avery's local collection were Earthly novels; some were documentaries; some were volumes of statistics about population densities, yeast production, and so on. It was not the most stimulating reading he'd ever done, but Derec read or viewed the documentaries—some were print, some audio-visual.

Presently he found that it was late and he was hungry, but he hesitated. "R. David, please check on Ariel and see if she is awake. If so, ask if she would like to accompany me to the section kitchen."

The robot did so, found her awake, and repeated the answer Derec had heard: "No, Mr. Avery, Miss Avery does not feel hungry and requires no food."

He hesitated about leaving her. If she felt hungry later, he could accompany her to the kitchen door, but doubted he'd be allowed in again tonight. Still, he could hang around outside and hope he wasn't questioned by a policeman. In any case, he himself was quite hungry despite his worry over Ariel.

He went out, stopping off at the Personal again and getting a drink from a public fountain outside it, then threaded the maze to the section kitchen. This time he got table J-10, and there was a longer wait; he saw that the room was near capacity. There weren't two adjoining spaces free at the table, as the Earthers tended to spread out as much as possible.

It was a gloomy meal, alone amid so many.

Then he retraced his weary route. *I suppose a person could get used to this,* he thought. *It's inconvenient, but you don't miss what you never had.* The Earthers obviously didn't give it a thought.

Questioned on this subject, R. David said, "It is not necessary for all Earth people to make this trek every time, of course. Holders of higher steps in each rating have such things as larger apartments, activated wash basins, subetherics, and so on. Of course, it is far more efficient to supply one section kitchen for four or five thousand households than to supply a room for cooking in each of these apartments, plus a cooker, food storage devices, food delivery, and so on. Just so with subetherics, when one big machine can replace a thousand small ones."

"But some people do have these things, and convenient laundry facilities in Personal, without having to go to the section laundry. Don't the have-nots resent these privileges?"

"Perhaps some do so, Mr. Avery, for humans are illogical. But human emotions are allowed for in the distribution of these favors, according to the Teramin Relationship."

"The what?"

"The Teramin Relationship. That is the mathematical expression that governs the differential between inconveniences suffered with privileges granted: dee eye sub jay taken to the—"

"Spare me the math; I'm a specialist in robotics, and even my math there is not fully developed. But I'm interested; I've never heard of any kind of math being applied to human relations. Can you express this Tera-whatchacallit Relationship verbally?"

"Perhaps an example would suffice, master. Consider that the privilege of having three meals a week in the apartment, even if the recipient has to fetch the meals himself from a section kitchen, if the privilege were granted for cause, will keep a large if varying number of people patient with their own inconveniences. For it demonstrates that privileges are real, can be earned without too great an effort, and have been earned by people whom one knows."

"Interesting," said Derec, thinking that the robots of Robot City ought to know this. "How do you know all this?"

"I aided Dr. Avery in his researches on society. I also aided him in his research into robotic history."

"Robotic history? On Earth?"

"But of course, Mr. Avery. The positronic brain, and the positronic robot, were invented on Earth. Susan Calvin was an Earthwoman, and Dr. Asenion an Earthman."

Those names he knew—Dr. Asenion, especially, the man who had codified the mathematics that expressed the Three

Laws in ways that made it possible to incorporate them into positronic brains. But Earth people! Still, it might explain much about Robot City. Dr. Avery was studying mass society and non-specialized robots on Earth.

"Is there a book on the mathematics of human society?" he asked, thinking it might well be good to take such a thing back to Robot City. Those poor robots had scarcely ever seen a human being, yet they were designed to serve mankind.

"I believe there are no Spacer books on the subject, Mr. Avery. However, I have several Earthly references of which you may have copies."

"I'd like that."

He'd like even more for Ariel to wake up and be her old self again. All during the afternoon he had had twinges of sharp fear, and kept trying not to remember that her disease was ultimately fatal.

Apparently everybody in Webster Groves had the idea of getting breakfast early; this was the worst jam yet. Ariel shifted from foot to foot and had the ungallant wish that Derec would carry her. Finally, however, they got in, made their way to their table, and sat with twin sighs.

The meal was lavish and included quite a few choices, including real meat sausages. Derec ate heavily, she saw, taking his own advice: it might be a long day. She tried to do so, but could not.

"I thought you were feeling better," he said.

"Yes," she said, and tried valiantly to eat more. How could she explain that her problem was as much psychological as physical? She had felt better this morning, but perhaps she was still feverish. Derec, in fact, had looked bad himself, as if he'd had another and worse nightmare. He'd said nothing.

"Just a claustrophobic attack," she muttered to him.

Derec nodded somberly.

It was partly that. Partly it was depression. Partly, she thought, it was sensory overload. Earth was so overwhelming! Even now—ten thousand jaws masticating food and the ceaseless din and motion around her—she wanted it all to *stop* for a minute, just for a minute! Even in her sleep, however, it never stopped.

And her illness was undoubtedly creeping up on her. If it crossed the blood-brain barrier, they had told her, it would be fatal. Until then she could still hope—dream—of a cure.

Well, the moments of inattention she had been experiencing, the fugues as she relived past memories only to lose them forever, the dreamlike hallucinatory state she often found herself in, could only mean one thing.

How could she tell Derec?

"Ready?"

Nodding, concealing her dread, Ariel rose and followed him out into yet more motion and noise.

The ways were surprisingly quiet, considering how many tons of people they carried, considering the speeds they moved at, considering the cleaving of the air over them. But the roar was always there under all consciousness, making Ariel feel more than ever that it was all a hallucination.

They retraced their route to Old Town Section, then through "Yeast Town," which began with East St. Louis Section. They sat, quiet, tense, through this section, but nobody paid any attention to them. Beyond, the sections stretched again, on and on to the east.

New York lay to the east, Derec had found, and he had no desire to try to drive around the City.

"Mommer!" yelled a young girl not far from them.

Derec and Ariel glanced at her apprehensively. It was rush hour, and all of them were standing, the Earthers patiently.

"Yeahr?" inquired an older woman, presumably Mommer. She wore a dark, baggy suit. The daughter wore a tight yellow one, over a rather unfortunate figure.

"'Member when Mayor Wong and all the Notables was at Busch Stadium 'time the Reds played?" she yelled.

"No," said Mommer, indifferently.

"'Member the girl that played the—" Ariel didn't get the title; it sounded like "star-mangled spanner"—"on the bugle?"

"Yeahr, so what?"

"That's my boyfriend Freddy's cousin Rosine!" the daughter shouted. She looked around triumphantly.

"No kiddin'?" Mommer asked, losing her indifference.

"'Swearta God!" cried the girl, looking around proudly, famous by contagion. "In fronta Wong an' all them Notables!"

At length, the lightworms overhead signaled END OF LINE. The crowd had thinned out long before, Mommer and daughter among the first to go. Only a few distinctly scruffy types were still on the ways. The edge of the City was evidently not a fashionable place. A number of men in obvious workmen's dress also rode with them.

The eastbound and westbound strips separated, were further divided by a building, and the strips tilted. At heart-stopping full speed the eastbound lane looped to the left, circled the building, and became the westbound lane. Ariel followed Derec down the strips just after the turn. He'd apparently been too interested to get off sooner.

"Oh, no!"

There was no crowd, and she thought that was the reason he got careless. Derec's foot came down on the join of two strips, and in a moment he'd been jerked off his feet. He rolled on his back down onto the slower strip.

Ariel leaped after him, in her haste not bracing herself, and fell forward at full length—fortunately, on the slower strip.

Derec, grunting, had rolled half onto a yet slower strip, which slipped from under his fingers as he clawed at it. With great presence of mind he rolled over yet again fully onto that strip.

Ariel hastily picked herself up and gingerly transferred to his new strip. Derec sat grinning faintly and watched her as she walked back toward him. A couple of Earthers glanced at them incuriously and looked up at the lightworms. Apparently falling riders weren't that uncommon. Nobody laughed.

Dusting himself off, Derec grinned more widely and led her down, then stopped in some consternation.

"Where's your purse?"

Ariel clapped a hand to her side, gasped. She didn't often

carry a purse, but had had to on Earth. With all the identification and such she had to carry here, it was a real necessity. Now it was all gone.

"No real matter—R. David can fake up more identification for you," Derec said.

They looked along the ways, but saw no sign of it. It must be hundreds of meters off by now, and they didn't know on which strip. Ariel shrugged.

"There must be some central office where you can reclaim things lost on the ways," Derec said, but dismissed it.

With a skill increased by their previous experiences, they made their way down into the bowels of the City to the freightway level. NO RIDING. PEDESTRIANS FORBIDDEN, the signs proclaimed. So they walked along beside them to the terminus, which was much like that of the passengerways above.

Small trucks with lifts in front and broad, flat beds behind brought in cannisters of freight. Somewhere not far from here big trucks were unloading these cannisters, driving in, wheeling out.

"Hey, you—you kids! Git away from there! Don't you see the sign? Go on, back!"

AUTHORIZED PERSONS ONLY.

Muttering, Derec led Ariel up a motionless ramp, hesitated, and struck out along a corridor running east. After half an hour of fruitlessly trying to go down to the entrance there, he retraced his steps and they went down to the lower level, and then marched toward the entrance. It was marked on the City maps as an entrance, not as an exit. There were no exits on the map.

NO ADMITTANCE TO UNAUTHORIZED PERSONS.

Derec opened the door cautiously, beckoned her through. Beyond it they found a garage for the handling trucks that transferred the cannisters. Men swarmed around it, but ignored them.

"We can't go there," Ariel said when he had led her behind the trucks to the motorway.

It was a stub motorway joining the entrance with the

freightway strips. To step out into that rumbling passage would be to get run over on the spot.

Derec hesitated. "Steal a handler and drive it out there?" he asked.

"And maybe keep on going?" she asked wistfully, thinking of sunlight and air. Tomorrow and New York were too far away to bother about. Her head hurt.

"No, we couldn't get much past the exit. These things are all beam-powered. That's why we have to have one of those big trucks. They're nukes."

In the end, they picked out a small handler and figured out the controls, which were quite simple.

"I'm surprised there's no control lock," said Ariel. "Knowing Earthly psychology."

"Frost, you're right," said Derec, worried, and looked it over. "This slot," he said after a moment. "For an ID tag, probably a specialized one." He looked it over and said, "I wish I had my tools."

Wonders can be performed with such things as metal ration tags. He worked away behind the control panel while Ariel crouched behind him in the tiny cab and watched anxiously for anyone approaching.

"Ready," he said at last. "Take the stick and drive us slowly out into the motorway."

She did so, nervously. At the door, the machine slowed, a panel on its controls lighting with the words: IDENTIFICATION REQUIRED BEYOND THIS POINT. Derec did something, a relay clicked quietly, and the handler rolled smoothly out into the stream.

"So far, so good," Derec said. "Nobody following."

Ariel turned to the right, guided them across the motorway to the proper lane, and they rolled slowly along toward the light. The traffic was fairly heavy, but moved slowly.

"Oh, almost—" Ariel said.

The light came from a vast open space where elephantine trucks trundled in and backed up to the loading docks. The handlers ran in and out of them, transferring their cargoes to small trucks, which took them to the freightways. Off to the right, a row of the huge trucks were disgorging golden grain into pipelines with a roar and a hiss of nitrogen.

"No good!" cried Derec. "Too many people. Pull over to the right, by those dumpsters. We'll pretend to be inspectors or something."

Sick, Ariel saw that he was right: There was little hope of seizing a truck unnoticed. The loading was done with smooth efficiency, though nobody seemed to move very fast. There were little knots of gossiping drivers and operators around. Men and women went around with clipboards, checking manifests. As soon as a truck was unloaded, it pulled out.

"Too bad we can't find a clipboard or two," Derec said.

Ariel thought that their shipsuits fit in pretty well, but wished they were cleaner. They had not thought to launder them—she had slept in hers, though the fabric didn't show it.

They got out of the handler reluctantly, and stood looking about.

Ariel yearned for the open. They could go to the edge of the dock, drop their own height to the concrete, and walk perhaps a hundred or a hundred fifty meters, and find themselves at the opening.

"Might have expected these Earthers to block off the opening," she observed. Light came in, but they couldn't see out.

"They don't even like as much of an opening as they've got," said Derec. "Notice how they all stand with their backs to it?"

They did. Each little group was a semicircle facing away from the opening.

"Let's go outside," she said impulsively.

Derec hesitated. "It might not be easy to explain. It might not be easy to get back in."

"Who wants to?" she said fiercely. "I just want to see sunlight one last time!"

Derec looked at her, frightened, concealed it, and said gently, "All right, we'll see what we can do."

He led her across the dock space and peered up at the numbers and letters on the side of one of the mammoth trucks. It was damp, and had dripped a puddle under it. Ariel had had no idea of how big they were till then. Nodding wisely, Derec stepped to the edge, turned, and dropped off.

Ariel followed.

They strode briskly, as if they had business there, toward the front of the truck. Beyond lay the barrier. Trucks entered obliquely between overlapping walls, so that vision could not reach out to the frightening openness outside but the trucks could enter without opening and closing doors. Ariel suspected that the way zigzagged, so great was the fear they showed of the outside.

"Hey! Hey, you two!"

A group of men were walking threateningly toward them on the docks, gesturing them back. One turned and dropped off as they watched. "Come back here!"

"Run!" said Derec.

A big wet truck erupted from the barrier even as they began to run, and they swerved. They found themselves running toward the grain trucks dropping their cargoes from their bellies.

A sign hovered in the air before them: WARNING: OXYGEN REQUIRED BEYOND THIS POINT!

Ariel remembered reading somewhere that grain dust could explode if liberally mixed with air. They stored it in nitrogen to prevent that. But, she observed, stricken with fear, the men working here were not wearing masks.

Derec led her on a route that avoided them—these workers looked up curiously but did not join the chase immediately—and they ran through the first dust cloud, then through the second.

"Not good enough," he said, as they paused, panting. Ariel tried not to cough; the dust was in her throat.

"Back up on the docks," she wheezed, and he nodded, led the way. With a grunt they were up, between trucks. The grain trucks didn't back up to the actual docks, which were quite narrow here. The whole area was fogged with dust.

They heard a shout, "Damn thieves," and looked back.

They had not been seen yet, but it was only a matter of time. The space beyond the dust cloud was a bedlam of whistles, shouts, and pounding feet. A big truck pulled away, its great wheels churning up more dust but making no sound.

A shout, something about laying the dust, came to them. Ariel couldn't get her breath. *We need oxygen,* she thought, and wanted to cough worse than ever. Out there they were coughing, too.

Red lights flamed overhead and a deep-toned horn sounded. Ariel looked up apprehensively to see yellow signs beside the red lights: SPRINKLERS . . . SPRINKLERS . . . SPRINKLERS. . . .

"Back in here, quick!" Derec cried, and pulled her back behind a tangle of implements, broken handler trucks, dust-bins, and the like.

Water spurted in a fine spray from the overhead, laying the dust immediately. A blue-clad man was among the truck drivers and dock workers; he carried a now-familiar club.

"A cop!" Derec said, groaning.

Ariel had glanced at him. And saw, beyond him—

"A door!"

"Where?"

"There, behind that tire."

The tire, a huge thing in bright-blue composition, discarded from one of the trucks, marked the end of the dump they were crouched in. There was a passageway by it to a small door.

In a moment they were trying it, and before the sprinklers cut off they were in a small, dim hallway with only one out of three lights burning.

PIPELINE CONTROL SECTION: NO ADMITTANCE TO UNAUTHORIZED PERSONS. But the hall led past. Farther on, they saw: GRAIN & BULK SUPPLY RATIO-NALIZING & BALANCING.

"Administrative controls on the basic levels," said Derec,

and Ariel thought of the men and women with clipboards.

"But there's nobody here," she said.

"Well, cities grow and change; these may be abandoned, or only needed periodically. The important thing is they may have access above—"

They did.

At the upper level, they found that they were far from the docks, to which they knew better than to return, but were not gone from the barrier yet. The motorways used by emergency vehicles also reached at least to the entry.

Beside the motorway was a pedestrian access door; the motorway door had no controls and probably opened by radio. Once through, walking nervously on the motorway, they found to their frustration that the way avoided the entrance, swooped, and dived down to the lower levels.

"It's for emergency vehicles," said Derec. "Ambulances, and so on. Accidents must be common on the docks."

Presently, they did find a half-concealed route that took them to the opening, and they looked out and down.

It was pouring with cold rain.

Even then Derec didn't give up, but Ariel's mind refused to record the details of the rest of the day. For several more hours he kept them prowling around the area, always trying to find a way to get at a big truck. But he could find no garage for them within the City and doubted seriously if there was one near to it.

Finally Ariel pleaded hunger and they gloomily rode the ways back to their section kitchen, able at least to sit down. Ariel felt doomed; one look at the cold gray rain falling endlessly outside had chilled her on some deep, basic level. She knew it was the last she'd ever see of the sky. For Derec, she felt sad, but was too tired to speak.

"We'll try again tomorrow at a different entrance," Derec said when she had eaten the little she could. "The sun will be shining—probably, anyway—and things will be all right."

She nodded indifferently.

CHAPTER 9
AMNEMONIC PLAGUE

To Derec's dismay, Ariel did not reappear that afternoon, and the next morning she arose late and looked terrible.

R. David became alarmed. "Miss Avery, you are not well. What are your symptoms?"

"The same as usual, R. David. Don't worry; I brought this illness with me; it's nothing to worry about." She sounded tired and fretful, trying not to worry his Three Law-dominated brain.

But a robot will worry if it seems appropriate, whether told not to or not. *They weren't so different from humans in that respect,* thought Derec, himself alarmed.

"I hope you are indeed not seriously ill, Miss Avery, but please tell me your symptoms so that I may judge. As you know, First Law compels me to help you."

She grimaced. "Okay. I'm frequently feverish—is there any water in the place?"

"No," Derec said. "I'll bring you—frost! is there anything to carry water in?"

"No," said R. David.

Mentally, Derec cursed all Earthers, individually and collectively, and the Teramin Relationship, too.

"Anyway, I'm often feverish, and tired and lethargic and listless. And—and—" she glanced at Derec. "I have mental troubles. Confusion—I forget where I am, lose track of what's going on. A lot of the time I sit and don't speak because I can't follow the conversation. I've been reliving the past a lot."

Suddenly she cried out passionately, "Nothing seems *real!* I feel like I'm in a hallucination."

It was more serious than Derec had thought. Hesitantly, he asked, "Do you feel like going to the section kitchen?"

"No. I don't feel like doing anything, except drinking a liter of water and going back to bed."

"You must go to section hospital at once," said R. David decisively, stepping forward.

Derec could have groaned. "What kind of medical care can you expect in an Earthly hospital?" he asked. "We've got to get you back to the Spacer worlds—"

"There's no cure for me there," she said quietly.

Damn. That was true. Derec hesitated, torn, and said, "Well, back to Robot City, then. Maybe the Human Medical Team has a cure."

"My medical knowledge is limited, primarily to the effects of Earthly ills on Spacers. But that knowledge makes me doubt that Miss Avery will—will live long enough for a space journey," said R. David, the catch in his voice obvious. "She is obviously in, or approaching, the—crisis of her disease."

Derec hesitated. That was too obviously true.

Ariel smiled sadly and said, "I fear he is right, Derec. I-I'm losing my memory—my mind. And it's getting worse. I couldn't remember my way back here the other night—"

Abruptly, she was weeping.

Oh, frost, Derec thought helplessly.

R. David gave them an argument; he wanted to accompany them—to carry Ariel, in fact.

"No!" said Derec. "I may be ignorant of many things about Earth, but I know well enough what Earthers do to any robots they catch on the ways. And if we tried to do anything about it, our first words would give us away as Spacers. They'd be all over us. I've been chased once by yeast farmers. Frost! I don't want to have *every* Earther we meet at our throats."

It took the firmest commands reinforcing Dr. Avery's to

keep R. David in the apartment. Only when Ariel perked up, as she usually did at the prospect of change, was the robot's First Law conditioning allayed. Ariel was even almost gay as she left, rendering a zany marching song: "One-two-three! Here we go! Bedlam, Bedlam, ho ho ho! Drrringding ding, brrrumbum bum, brrrreebeedeebee Dabbabba-dum-bum-bum!"

But once the door had closed she looked haggard.

"Water," she said, smiling wanly at Derec's concerned look.

After she had drunk a liter or so, she gasped for breath a few minutes, but was game to go on. The route to the section hospital was longer than the one to the kitchen, and she drooped visibly. Worse, it was morning now and the express was jammed. They had to stand; Threes weren't allowed to sit during rush hour.

It seemed that the nightmare of rushing ways and whistling wind and unconcerned, self-centered Earthers would go on forever. Derec had to watch Ariel—he feared she would collapse—and also watch the signs overhead, fearing that he would forget or confuse the instructions he had carefully impressed on his memory.

But even the longest journey ends at last, and the exit was clearly marked SECTION HOSPITAL, with the same red cross on white that Spacers used.

The anteroom smelled of antiseptic and was mobbed with men, women, and children. *Children,* thought Derec vaguely—*never seen so many children in my life as on Earth.* Though his memories still were lost, he was sure, by his astonished reaction, that he had not. Of course, they had to keep replacing this huge population.

Fumbling, he inserted Ariel's newly forged ID tags into the computer, whose panel lit with CHECK-UP, ILLNESS, EMERGENCY? Ariel was leaning against him, gasping and pale after the ordeal, and even the usually unconcerned Earthers were looking at them in some alarm. Emergency, he decided, panicky, and punched it.

Instantly a red star appeared in the panel, blinking; apparently alarms rang elsewhere, for a strong-looking woman appeared, started to remonstrate with him for mistaking an ILLNESS for an EMERGENCY—young husbands! But Ariel turned a ghastly, apologetic smile on her, and the woman's mouth closed with a snap.

"Here!"

She half carried Ariel past three rooms full of still more waiting Earthers, to a room with a wheeled, knee-high cart in it.

"Lie down, baby!"

The gurney stood up, she strapped Ariel on, and an older woman entered. "Dr. Li—"

"Mmm. I see." She began to check over Ariel, not bothering with instruments—she took Ariel's temperature by placing her hand on Ariel's head!

A harassed-looking man entered. He wore a curious ornament in the form of a frame holding glass panes in front of his eyes. Derec had noticed some of these on the ways. It gave his face a dashing, futuristic look. "What is it, Dr. Li?"

"Don't know yet, Dr. Powell. Elevated temperature, febrile heartbeat, hectic flush, exhaustion. I want to measure everything first, of course." She reached to the bottom of the gurney and started pulling out instruments, to Derec's considerable relief. Ariel had closed her eyes, and seemed to be asleep.

The doctors bent over her, shaking their heads and measuring everything about Ariel. Tense as he was, Derec looked about for a place to sit, content for the moment to leave it in their hands. Abruptly the nurse said. "How long has it been since she's eaten?"

The doctors ignored this till Derec said, "Uh—yesterday afternoon. Not long after noon."

Dr. Li grunted, and Dr. Powell said, "Inanition!"

"Young as she is, that shouldn't have brought on this collapse. Feel that arm. She's practically starving." The three of them looked at each other, plainly shocked.

"Why hasn't she been eating, young man?" Dr. Li demanded.

"She hasn't felt like it, Ma'am," said Derec, and all three of them frowned at his accent.

"Settler prospects, eh?" Powell removed his frame and wiped the panes with a tissue. "You'll not have much need of Spacer talk on a frontier planet. Better to learn some good medieval jargon: brush, creek, log cabin. Not to mention 'sweat.' What's wrong with her?"

"I don't know, Doctor. She said," he gulped, "it could be fatal if it crossed the blood-brain barrier. It's—it's affecting her mind. She's had th-this low-level fever and lethargy, with occasional muscular aches and pains, for a long time."

"Vomiting? Night sweats?" asked Dr. Li tensely.

"I don't know. She-she didn't want to worry me."

They looked outraged; he should *know*.

"There's a number of things it could be," said Dr. Li unhappily. "I have a few ideas, though—"

"So do I!" said Dr. Powell sourly. "Look here, young fella, I don't doubt that accent caused you many a pain, but you'd better doff it in here. It antagonizes too many people."

"He can't," said Dr. Li expressionlessly. "He's a real Spacer."

Dr. Powell and the nurse goggled. "Impossible! A Spacer running around on Earth? He'd drop down dead of—"

The doctors whirled to look at Ariel. Frowning, the nurse stepped out. "It could be any of a hundred common and harmless diseases!" said Dr. Powell.

"Yes! Harmless to Earth people!"

"How about yourself, young man? Do you feel all right?" Derec nodded. "Never better."

"Why, then?" Dr. Powell exploded. "You should be sick a dozen times over!"

"I've been given a prophylactic regimen—so has Ariel," said Derec, hoping they wouldn't ask too many questions. "I don't know too much about it."

"Apparently it didn't take in her case," said Dr. Li somberly. "You let us know the moment you feel unwell, young man."

"They can't be Spacers," said the nurse grimly, holding

Ariel's ID tag in her hand. "How could they be, and travel around Earth? Without ration cards, ID, and so on? This is perfectly ordinary Earth ID, City of St. Louis—"

They looked at him, frowning harder, and Derec felt himself hot . . . not to mention sweating. "That's all arranged, sir. It's part of a trade agreement . . . we're doing sociological research . . ."

"So young?"

"Who notices a kid?" he countered swiftly, feeling the hair clammy against his forehead. "Young eyes see more sharply . . . and so on."

"Hummph! No child of mine would take such a risk—"

"Maybe we'd better query the Terries," said Dr. Li reluctantly.

They all looked concerned.

Derec questioned them with his eyes, but finally had to break down and ask. "The who?"

"The Terries—Terrestrial Bureau of Investigation," said Dr. Powell. He polished his panes unhappily.

"They cause more trouble than—" muttered the nurse.

"Still, best to take no chances. If the girl is in a bad way, it could cause trouble with the Spacers—there's enough bad blood between us already."

Derec thought swiftly, appalled. The "Terries" would find no record of them, would query whatever Spacer representation there might be on Earth, find no record there, and the reactor would flash over. But he couldn't think of a thing to say.

"Look—"

Ariel moaned and turned partly on her side; only the straps kept her from falling. If she'd been listening, she couldn't have timed it better. All three Earthers leaped to her, and Derec pocketed the ID tag the nurse had put down.

He thought quickly. The doctors were concerned and totally focused on Ariel. Derec looked around. As he recalled R. David's work, the ID tag merely gave name and ID workup. Not address. Medical care was on an as-needed basis, not rationed, so nobody cared about place of residence, and in fact they hadn't been required to enter that. (Or was that because Ariel's tag gave her rating as Transient? He needed to know a lot more about Earth.)

In any case, he thought, the only thing they knew about Ariel was what the computer recorded from the ID tag.

Leaving them working over her, he slipped out and strolled around, speaking to no one, trying to look like a worried, expectant father pretending to be nonchalant. A couple of people looked at him sympathetically, but most didn't seem to notice him at all, for which he was grateful.

There it was. An office. He slipped in, looked at the terminal. It was probably dedicated to a single function, but he could try. He had watched R. David coding ID tags of a dozen kinds, and had a good grasp of what was implied. And frankly, these computers were simple after programming positronic brains and restructuring the programming of the central computer of Robot City. It took him a mere half hour to get through the programming, retrieve the record on Ariel, and erase it.

Now let's hope there isn't a backup memory somewhere, he thought gloomily.

They caught up with him in the interior waiting room, standing aimlessly about and unobstrusively slipping toward the outer waiting room, where he supposed he belonged.

"There you are," said the nurse. For the first time, he noted that her jacket had a name label imprinted *Korolenko, J.* "Why didn't you wait in the Friends' Lounge?"

He didn't bother to tell her they hadn't shown him to it. "Had to go to the Personal," he said, not knowing if Earthers could mention the Personal so openly.

She got ideas, frowned, put something warm from her pocket against his head. Apparently his temperature was all right. "Very well. But come in here. The doctors will need to speak to you."

Within ten minutes Dr. Li entered the room briskly, sat down, exhaled heavily. "She had us worried, but it was mostly exhaustion of the body's resources. Starvation, to put it crudely. She must have been going on nerves and caffeine for weeks."

"She hasn't been eating well," Derec admitted. He'd been blind not to see how little she'd been eating. "What does she have?"

"We'll know for sure in a day; we've done a culture. But our best guess is amnemonic plague."

"Ay . . . nuhmonic . . . ?"

"From medieval *mnemonic*, meaning memory. Amnemonic means no memory. It's a mutation of an old influenza virus, first reported on one of the Settler worlds—sometimes called Burundi's Fever, after the discoverer." She looked at him sharply, but clearly that name meant no more to Derec than the first.

"Will she—get better?"

Dr Li sighed. "When Burundi's crosses the blood-brain barrier, it isn't good. We're giving her support—nourishment and so on—and antibiotics that eventually will cure the disease. Our anti-virals are fairly effective, except where the virus has crossed the blood-brain barrier. Antibodies will help a little, and we're administering them. We'll be able to stop the infection in all but her brain within a day or two."

Derec had the illusion that his chest had turned into a block of wood. His heart pushed once, hard, against its unyielding surroundings, and gave up. He felt it stop moving. "Her . . . brain?"

Dr. Li sighed and looked four hundred years old. "There's hope. It's by no means over. I do *wish* we'd gotten at her sooner. . . . Well, try not to feel guilty; and I'm sorry if I made you feel worse. You couldn't have known. All kids are heedless, think they'll live forever. . . ." She brooded on her capable hands for a moment.

"Then you think she'll live?"

"Let's say, I have a good hope of it. Saul—Dr. Morovan —is a specialist on viruses and has treated amnemonic plague three times, twice successfully—and the third time was a patient whose disease had advanced much farther than your wife's."

Derec suspected that the symptoms of the other two had been much less advanced than Ariel's, but said nothing. It was something, he acknowledged, that they knew the disease, had a cure for it, and had hope for her. *Of course,* he thought, *we were fools—chauvinistic fools—to assume that the Spacer worlds were the only ones that knew anything about medicine.* Who but Earth, incubator of virtually every disease known to mankind, would know more about medicine? Among the Spacer worlds, he supposed, amnemonic plague was invariably fatal when it crossed the blood-brain barrier. . . .

Derec felt his knees shaking and was glad he wasn't standing.

"What?" He'd missed some of what she'd been saying.

"Need a sample," she repeated. "We can't give you the vaccine if you have the disease, at least in its later stages."

The Key to Perihelion affected the stomach like this: a sudden drop as one went from gravity to free-fall instantly. Derec nearly threw up. Gulping, he said, "Y-yes, Ma'am," and held out his arm.

Disease!

The possibility had always been there, associating with Ariel. But it was obvious that what she had wasn't easily contagious. She had only mentioned once, more or less directly, how she had contracted her illness, as a warning to him. But that was the only time they had come close to more than accidental physical contact. Now that he thought about it, she had kept her distance, even when she had clearly wanted and needed to be hugged. His Spacer's horror of disease had not been as greatly allayed as he had thought, he realized, shaky. The prophylactic treatment R. David had given them had reassured him, Ariel's attitude and his worry over her had reassured him, and the heedlessness of youth. . . .

His eyes must have mirrored some of his horror, for Dr.

Li looked at him sharply and said, "Don't worry! You're obviously in a very early stage, if you have it at all. And we're going to give you a thorough going-over, to make sure you aren't coming down with something else."

They did that for the next half hour. *The Human Medical Team would have been faster, but no less thorough,* he thought.

"Good, you're totally free of disease, so far as we can tell," said Dr. Powell. "Fortunately, your intestinal microorganisms are not markedly different from the Terrestrial strains, and there's as yet nothing else to worry about. Dr. Li, the vaccine. . . . "

"Incidentally, we detected antitoxins to Burundi's in your system," said Dr. Li. "You may have had a mild case of the fever earlier; it may even still be latent in your system. However, the vaccine will immunize you totally."

"Uh—" said Derec, as a thought took him. "Have I been a carrier all this time?"

Uneasily, he visualized Ariel and himself spreading disease all over Rockliffe Station, where they had crashlanded after escaping the pirate Aranimas. Any human who subseqently entered the station might contract the disease—

"Perhaps, but don't worry about it. Amnemonic plague is misnamed; it isn't a true plague. It's not infectious at all, and only minimally contagious. You have to exchange actual body fluids; it's commonly passed in sexual intercourse, or in contaminated blood supplies. And occasionally by poorly sterilized hypodermics, out on the Settler worlds where they have to reuse their needles."

That was a relief. But it left a puzzle: how had Derec been exposed to the disease, if not from breathing the air around Ariel? Had he had it *before* he'd met her on Aranimas's ship?

He must have. How else had he lost his memory? But how, then, had he survived? If amnemonic plague only affected the memory after passing the blood-brain barrier, and among Spacers was invariably fatal when it did—

Again he had missed something.

"I said, your wife is almost certainly going to live. Here, catch him!"

Derec didn't know who did what; his vision had momentarily blanked. When the light came back, he was sitting and there was a tingle in his arm; *a stimulant spray,* he thought vaguely. They were proffering a glass of orange juice to him—perfectly normal orange juice, just like the oranges of Aurora. He wondered how much it had cost to ship it here, then realized that they must have bought orange tree seedlings sometime in the past, and raised their own.

"Thank you," he whispered.

They stood around and watched him intently.

"Is there something?"

"Yes," said Dr. Li reluctantly. "I hope you're up to this. It . . . may upset you."

Derec took another swallow of the juice, marveling again that it could be so exactly like Auroran juice. "I'm braced," he said. "Go ahead."

"Amnemonic plague is well-named, though it's no plague. Your wife is losing her memory, and at a progressive rate. By the time we've cured her, there won't be much of it left."

CHAPTER 10
THE KEY TO MEMORY

Derec lay on the hard, narrow bed and wondered what Wolruf and Mandelbrot were doing. Probably still sitting out around Kappa Whale in the Star Seeker, waiting, waiting. Of course, they could not readily get space charts without a human to front for them, though Mandelbrot might try. It would not be unusual for a robot to open communications. But if the other ship insisted on speaking to the owner-captain —Star Seekers were small ships; he couldn't very well be far from the controls. For that matter, Derec was uncertain how well Mandelbrot could lie in such circumstances.

Well, there was nothing he could do for them. He couldn't leave Earth, and if he could, he couldn't leave Ariel here. And Ariel was now raving in delirium in the section hospital in Webster Groves Sector, City of Saint Louis. A long way, he gathered, from the nearest spaceport, near New York.

Derec wished for a drink. He wished for a light snack, cookies at least, and fresh hot coffee, even synthetic coffee. In the next room was a robot, ready to spring into action at his slightest word—almost. It was an Earthly robot, in an Earthly City. Derec could send R. David out, but there was no assurance it would return—and it would not be with food, for Derec didn't rate meals in his own apartment. Damn Dr. Avery for not arranging for higher ratings.

But that would have been more conspicuous, he supposed.

Light from the door shone across the bed. "Time to arise, Mr. Avery," said R. David.

"Yes, thank you, R. David."

Derec groaned silently and sat up to sit for a moment with his elbows on his knees, chin in hands. In the short life that he could remember, it had been one crisis after another. All I want, he decided, is peace and quiet, a little establishment on some mountain brook in the boondocks of Aurora or Nexon, maybe, with just a couple of robots and a landing field only big enough for my own machine and one other. Maybe the Solarians had the right idea; they never saw *any-body,* and lived totally surrounded by robots.

No, he had decided. That wasn't such a good idea, after all.

Earth turned inside out, he thought vaguely. No better than—

"Mr. Avery, are you well?"

"Yes, R. David. Merely depressed. I worry about Ariel."

That, the robot could well understand.

"Yes, Mr. Avery. I—also worry about her. But the doctors report her condition good, do they not?"

"Yes, they did last night, R. David. What she's like today—" He left it, somber, dressed carelessly, and tucked some equipment into the little bath satchel he had bought the day before.

Admonishing R. David rather hollowly not to worry, he set off for the Personal, returned to drop off the satchel when he had showered and washed his extra clothing, and departed for the section kitchen. This part of the trip was so routine now that he neither saw nor was seen by the policemen in the corridors and junctions; he no longer stood out like a stranger.

Breakfast was, as usual, good, but to him, tasteless. Listlessly, Derec ate it, not even interested in a fact he had finally deduced: it was neither synthetic nor natural, but both. It was made of living things and was therefore natural, but was made by an artificial process and was therefore synthetic. The basis of three-quarters of it was yeast.

He suspected that there might be a steady, if small, market for Earthly food yeasts in the Spacer worlds, if Spacers could overcome their sense of superiority long enough to try it. Granted, Spacer high cuisine had no equal on Earth that Derec had tasted, but Spacer ships were usually furnished with synthesizers. *So much for Spacer cuisine,* he thought.

The hospital was a familiar place to him now. Derec did not trouble with the waiting rooms, but went to the Friends' Lounge and queried Ariel's condition on the monitor. There had been a problem with that when they had discovered that she wasn't in the system. Derec had professed ignorance of the ID tag, and it was assumed—he hoped—that it had been lost when they all crowded around to help Ariel during her collapse.

Naturally he didn't remember her number, and in their honest ignorance she and he had left other ID forms behind. Derec had promised to supply them with it next day, but so far had "forgotten" to do so the one time they remembered to ask him for it. They had had to input her with a dummy ID.

Ariel was in a room with two robots. Here, in Intensive Care, people were either unconscious or so debilitated by their illnesses that they didn't care that it was robots who waited on them.

She was not raving today. At first Derec thought she was asleep, she lay so quietly. But then she moved, and a robot sprang forward to smooth the pillow behind her. She looked at it vacantly, closed her eyes.

A faint sound behind him was Dr. Li. The woman shook her head sadly.

"How is she, doctor?" Derec asked.

"As far as the disease goes, the worst is over. She will live. But what you're seeing now might be worse. She is gradually losing her memories."

Derec had had some of this explained to him. "I suppose she's half in a hallucinatory state now."

"Yes, or something like an intense daydream. Perhaps a

brown study would be a better analogy—one of those almost hypnotic states of concentration in which you don't see
what's in front of you."

Derec had a vague flash memory of someone waving a
hand in front of his nose, and nodded.

Ariel was reliving her life as drowning people are popularly supposed to do. *It wouldn't take me long,* he mused; *I
suppose I might have time for it. But Ariel. . . .*

"Could I visit her?"

Dr. Li frowned, looking sadder. "You could, but after
today it will get worse." She hesitated. "There's always a
shock for the loved ones, when the patient doesn't recognize
them. That will happen, you know."

Derec hadn't thought of that, and the mere thought
shocked him. "Then—can I visit her today?"

"I'll ask."

Ariel looked at him blankly, but it wasn't a lack of recognition. It was more a lack of energy. "Oh, Derec. How are
you?"

What do you say to someone who may be alive tomorrow, but won't remember you? If Derec's memories had
been a hundred years long rather than a couple of months, he
still wouldn't have had anything to guide him.

"Well enough," he said awkwardly. He drew near to the
bed, touched it. She looked at him without much emotion.

"Are you going to help them restore my memory?"

"Of course. I'll have to. And I hope you've been talking—?" He indicated the robots with a tilt of his head.

"A little," she said reluctantly. "I'm so tired all the time.
And they keep me so full of drugs I don't have the spirit.
Besides, it doesn't matter. It won't help. It w-won't really be
me. Derec, it's like dying. It's just like dying. I won't see
you again—I won't see anyone again—it's all fading—"

One of the robots sprang to the head of the bed and did
something, and Ariel's eyes closed. When they opened after
a moment the horror had largely passed. Derec thought it
was still there, though, masked by the drug.

"That isn't so, Ariel," he said insistently. "Your memories are still there, in your brain. They merely need to be unlocked. We'll—"

She was shaking her head. "No, it's all going. I'm dying, Derec. Whoever takes my place will be someone different."

Abruptly he said, "Am I different than—the man I was?"

"Of course. And yet, you're him." She closed her eyes and tears trembled on her eyelids. The robot got busy at the headboard again.

"Derec, I want you to know that I've always loved you. Even when I was most angry, even when I was most frightened. I never blamed you. For weeks I've watched, hoping you would never develop the final form of the disease. I guess you did, or you wouldn't have lost your memory. Whoever cured you...didn't have the...technology to restore...your memory..."

She drifted off into sleep, and after a moment Derec choked down his impulse to cry out, to demand that they awaken her. Suddenly his lost memory seemed less important, what she knew seemed less important, than what she thought of him.

"Farewell, Ariel," he managed to say huskily, and stumbled out into the Friends' Lounge, where he sat and wept for a time, quietly. He wondered vaguely if, in all his unremembered life, he had felt this sharp, poignant pain, and doubted it. Yet, he had known her in another life, and it had not been wholly a happy relationship.

He'd had amnemonic plague; the emptiness in his head was proof enough for him. Had he gotten it from her—or given it to her?

Presently he took a deep breath, let it out in a sigh that came from the bottom of his belly, and wiped his face on a tissue from the dispenser. Robots were probably watching him; within minutes Dr. Li and a weary-looking Dr. Powell entered the room.

They sat and looked him over while he braced himself. Fortunately, they, like he, had more important things on their minds than Ariel's ID tags.

"I understand that Korolenko has told you a little about

memory restoration," Dr. Powell said.

Derec remembered an exchange from an earlier visit. He nodded. "Memory traces are not memory. Yes."

"Quite so. A memory trace is the synapse—the nerve connection in the brain—that leads to the memory, which is stored in chemical form. It is these synapses that are being erased by the neurotoxin of the plague. The actual memories remain untouched."

They looked at him. *If only you knew how much I know about this,* he thought. "Right," he said. "But since their addresses are unknown—to put it in computer jargon—the memories are as lost as if the records *had* been wiped."

"Almost," said Dr. Li. "There are ghost memories flitting about the patient's mind, and many little things will jolt a few of the memories loose."

"Smell is one of the subtlest and most powerful memory keys," said Dr. Powell, nodding.

Derec knew. "Yes."

"So. In what we loosely call a memory restoration, we merely supply new synapses as nearly identical to the old as possible."

"And in the functioning of the new memory traces," Derec said, parroting what he'd been told, "the patient reactivates the old chemical memories."

"Quite so. The more accurate and detailed the new memory traces are, the more complete not only the restoration of the memories, but the restoration of the patient's original *personality*. I hope you can see that."

It was an angle that had never occurred to him. He supposed he had the same basic personality as ever: pragmatic, problem-solving, not given to abstract thought, not artistic or poetic. An equable temperament. The engineering mind.

Now that he thought of it, though, perhaps his personality was different. He had known Ariel in his former life. He must have had strong feelings about her. He did again. Not still—*again*. For if he had not met her since his memory loss, and had not continuously been practically in solitary confinement with her, he might well not have felt that way about her again.

His parents, for instance. He no longer felt about them as he once must have done. His friends—all those parts of his personality were gone. If he acquired new friends, his emotional responses would be much the same, of course. His personality had not changed in any *basic* way, or so he supposed. He did not seem very strange to Ariel. Still, he was a new and different person from the old Derec, whatever his name had been.

Perhaps Ariel was right; perhaps it was a form of death.

Yet— "If the memory traces are close enough to the original—?"

"Ideally, it would be like copying a program into a blank positronic brain," said Dr. Li. "The second robot would, for all practical purposes, *become* the old one."

"We always explain what's been done to them," Derec said absently.

"Yes. But if the original was destroyed—" Derec frowned. "—the new one would, for all intents and purposes, be the same one in a new body."

True, it was not unlike shifting a positronic brain to a new robotic body. Derec had an uneasy flash. On Robot City there had been an accidental death, of a boy called David, which Derec and Ariel had investigated for the robots. This David had looked just like him—

He usually shrugged that fact off, but now he was jolted. Maybe the other was the duplicate—or was it himself?

"In a human, of course, it is not quite so simple," said Dr. Powell, not noticing his jolted expression. "We could activate a significant fraction of the locked memories without reactivating the old personality. It's a matter of knowing which memories are *important* to the patient."

"How close can we come?" Derec asked.

"It depends on how much we know. The robots are, of course, recording and analyzing everything she says, and there's a tendency to relive the most important memories first and most often, till they're gone. So we're developing a good sketch, too crude to be called a diagram."

Derec nodded. "That's where you need my help."

"Quite so. You know her better than we, or the robots, can hope to."

"Not well enough, I'm afraid," said Derec steadily, wishing for some of that tranquilizer they were keeping Ariel on. "I've only known her for a few weeks."

And already married, their expressions said. Spacer morals. Derec didn't enlighten them. "I can go into a lot of detail about our time together, but before that . . . she was a very private person."

Again, their expressions spoke for them: *Spacers lived alone, on the surface, surrounded only by robots, and had few human contacts. . . .* Not true, but try to explain. Besides, he'd had his own quota of chauvinistic nonsense about Earthers to lose.

"Whatever you can do, you must do," Dr. Li said heavily.

"Uh . . . well . . . I can't," Derec said lamely.

If he mentioned his amnesia, they'd be all over him. The question of their identities would arise in a way he couldn't duck. The Terries would certainly be called in, and the Spacer embassy at the port would be queried. The whole house of cards would come down—next thing you knew, they'd have learned about Dr. Avery—and Robot City.

That secret must be kept at all costs.

"Why not?" Dr. Powell barked.

"It's . . . a matter of privacy, sir."

"Oh." Greatly mollified. Spacers! "Well, there's a lot more than you could do sitting here . . . why don't you take all the material we have with you, go home, and do your dictating there?"

Derec had been so used to having First Law-driven robots intruding on his life that he was startled by this easy acquiescence. A robot wouldn't let anything be put into Ariel's head without checking it over first.

"And the memory traces? Will they be kept private?"

The doctors looked at each other. "Well, they have to be coded," Dr. Li began.

Dr. Powell said, "They use a technique modified from one used to implant synapses in positronic brains. Of course that can't be used on human brains, but it's based on the same idea, as it were. I don't know the full details, myself—"

"But it's a matter of coding," said Dr. Li. "We're having a specialist come in from the Mayo. If he could teach you— perhaps you could code the more private portions . . .?"

It took several conversations and a conference before it was decided to let Derec attempt coding memory traces for Ariel. His education stood him in good stead; he had the necessary background to do the work. *Spacer!* said the expressions again, this time with approval. Spacer education in robotics and computers in general was notoriously the best.

The work called for the use of a good computer, and with some trepidation he revealed the existence of R. David during the conference.

"Of course," Dr. Powell said. "A Spacer would naturally have a robot in his apartment."

They seemed to take it quite for granted, and to be a little amused by it.

"Scots sleeping with bagpipes," someone muttered at the back of the room, a reference that sounded so funny that Derec meant to look it up, but forgot. He didn't think of it again till weeks later . . . far too late to ask.

So, once he was instructed in the technique—not simple, but not too hard to learn—of coding memories as synapses, Derec sat up, day and night, dictating his memories of his life with Ariel.

"Any time she remembers something, playing the memory trace, there is a certain strong chance that she will unlock the actual memory of the event, or of part of it," the expert told Derec. "Each such unlocked memory will be retained, and will strengthen the memory trace leading to it, and to the fields about it. All this was worked out at the

Lahey within the past ten years."

She was a sharp-nosed, unpretty woman, tiny and quite dark of skin. The breeds of mankind, or races as they were called on Earth, remained far more distinct than on the Spacer worlds. Darla, her name was, and she knew her stuff. She seemed to be hundreds of years old; he supposed vaguely that she might be sixty or seventy.

"Eventually, the personality that is recovered will be indistinguishable from the patient's original personality, both to the patient and to the patient's loved ones. But that depends on the accuracy of the memories, the accuracy of the coding, and the completeness of the memories."

The coding accuracy he could create by care and sheer hard work. The completeness of the memories he had little control over. *At least,* he thought comfortingly, *the last weeks of her life must be very important,* and those he could cover well.

But the accuracy of the memories? How did he know what was important to her and what was not? Her moods had always been a mystery to him.

He could but do his best, and try not to worry too much.

Derec took to visiting the hospital every other day, and sometimes every third day. Whether he went or not, he always stopped at the public combooth mornings and evenings, on the way to and from the kitchen, to call and ask about her. The news usually was that she was doing well but was in no condition to talk.

Derec knew it. His work went rapidly enough, but there was a lot of it. He slogged through it grimly. If not for the necessity of going out to call the hospital, he might not have gone near the kitchen until R. David was forced to take action to prevent collapse.

He had one slight consolation. His own memories must also be locked away, unharmed by the plague. If only he could find someone who knew him as well as Ariel did before she lost her memories, someone he could persuade to come to Earth and dictate his memories . . . not likely, knowing Spacers. But there was that thread of hope that he might recover his memories . . . might recover himself.

Nights were bad. He dreamed nightmares of Ariel not responding to the treatment and being as blank as he had been upon awakening. It was terribly important that she not lose her memories of him . . . and in the dream it was always his fault. His coding failed, or she was swept away in the flash floods through the drains of Robot City, or. . . .

Robot City! It, too, haunted his dreams, and these dreams were even darker and more frightening than the nightmares about Ariel. Those he could understand; they sprang from a quite natural anxiety.

But the Robot City dreams were different . . . they didn't even seem like dreams. They seemed frighteningly real. In the mornings Derec's hands shook, and he hoped the doctors never started asking serious questions. They'd know for sure he was crazy.

He was dreaming that Robot City was *inside* him. He dreamed of gleaming buildings rising on the lobes of his liver, great dark-red plains stacked above each other, or on his ribs, or inside his lungs, the buildings expanding and contracting as he breathed. Then the dreams seemed to become much clearer, and he "knew," in the crazy dream way, that Robot City was in his bloodstream.

Enclosed buildings, like space cities on lonely rocks, he thought. Yeah! But jeering didn't drive off the frightened, helpless feeling, the feeling of being invaded and used.

I suppose that's the source of this dream, he thought, trying to comfort himself. *I've been moved and manipulated from the beginning.*

The next time he walked into the Friends' Lounge, Korolenko brought him Dr. Li and an unsmiling, athletic young man with the look of eagles in his eyes.

"Yes?" Derec said to the stranger.

"This is Special Agent Donovan," said Dr. Li, frowning slightly. "Of the Terrestrial Bureau of Investigation."

CHAPTER 11
QUESTIONS!

The Terry followed him and Dr. Li to a more private conference room, where Dr. Li left them.

The special agent looked Derec over intently, but not in a hostile manner. Derec braced himself, shaky. Above all, he mustn't mention Robot City. Neither could he mention Aranimas and Wolruf. They'd consider him crazy.

Any break in his story would mean endless questioning, queries to the Spacer worlds, questions about Dr. Avery, the discovery of Wolruf in orbit about Kappa Whale, perhaps the discovery of all that Dr. Avery was doing . . . not all of that bad, but it would take time! Worst of all, the investigation would ultimately uncover Robot City . . . and that secret had to be kept at all costs.

Derec and Ariel had to get back there.

"I must warn you that this conversation is being recorded, and that anything you say may be used against you. Further, you have the right to remain silent, if you feel that your interests might be threatened by answering. On the other hand, we have as yet no positive evidence that any crime has been committed. The Bureau has been called in primarily because you are allegedly a Spacer . . . diplomatic reasons, that is,"

Derec nodded, throat tight.

"Who are you?" the agent asked abruptly.

"Derec."

"And your last name?"

Derec debated, decided not, and said, "I sit mute."

"That is your right. Do you wish a witness that you have not been coerced?"

"Waived, but, uh," Derec could not quite remember the Spacer legal formula—so far it had seemed close to Earth's. If anything, Earth was more fanatical about preserving the individual's rights than the Spacer worlds were. "Uh, I wish to retain the right to ask for a witness later."

"Waived right to a witness pro tem," said Donovan, nodding shortly once, in faint approval. "I assume then that you do not mean to sit mute to all questions. Therefore, I ask you: have you ever had Burundi's disease, popularly known as amnemonic plague?"

"I don't remember." Derec smiled faintly at the other and received a faint smile back.

"Do you remember your last visit to Towner Laney Memorial Hospital, two days ago, and the blood sample that was taken at that time?"

Derec remembered the visit, but not the blood sample. Even when Donovan pointed at the red scab inside his left elbow, he still didn't remember the sample being taken. .

Concerned, Donovan said, "Do you assert that it was taken without your knowledge; particularly, do you accuse anyone of using anesthesia on you against your will?"

"Is that a crime on Earth? No, I make no such—uh—assertion. I just don't remember . . . I was probably in a fog. I usually am, these days."

The agent looked at him. "Isn't unauthorized anesthesia a crime on the Spacer worlds?"

"It might be, but I doubt it. I doubt that it happens often enough for anyone to pass a law against it. The robots would prevent it, usually."

"Hmmm," said the Terry, possibly reflecting that a robot-saturated society might have its points. "In any case, I now inform you that a blood sample was taken from you on that occasion and carefully studied. The conclusion of the doctors here, and at the Mayo, and in Bethesda, is that though you have antitoxins to Burundi's, you have never had the disease in its severe form."

Derec stared at him.

Donovan continued, "Yet, something you said to the Spacer plague victim, and which she answered, indicates that your memory was lost in the characteristic fashion of this disease. Can you elucidate that, or do you wish to sit mute?"

The robots, thought Derec. Furniture to a Spacer, he had paid no attention. And usually a robot's discretion was proverbial, so much so that their testimony was rarely heard even in Spacer courts. But these had been instructed to record and play back everything that Ariel said. Derec couldn't remember what she and he had said, but they'd given the game away more than an Earthly week ago.

Had they mentioned Robot City?

"Why do you ask?" he asked warily.

"Do you suffer from amnesia?" the other countered.

Derec ought to sit mute. He considered that seriously, wondered if perhaps it was already too late, then thought of a possible way around.

"Why do you ask? Surely it's no crime to suffer amnesia. Nor would I expect the Terries to be called in even if a Spacer suffered. The condition isn't contagious, you know."

"There are laws against harboring certain diseases, nevertheless," said Donovan automatically, but he waved that aside. "Public policy. No, the question here is more serious. Essentially, two things about you alarm us. One is that you do not remember your past. The other is that you are not on Earth."

Derec gaped at him, almost started to ask exactly where St. Louis was.

"Officially, I mean," said Donovan, frowning in irritation. "We've done a thorough computer check, and we find no sign of you before you appeared here a couple of weeks ago, eating at the section kitchen, big as life and twice as natural. This was brought to our attention by the hospital's accountants and computer operators, who have never discovered how your partner's records vanished out of the hospital's computer."

The Terry looked at him again. "Normally I wouldn't reveal so much, but there's a good deal of alarm in Washington. It's considered that you are not the source of the mystery, and may in fact be unaware of it. Who sent you to Earth, and why?"

Derec's mind was spinning like a wheel, but he managed to say, "I suppose you figure the ones who sent us have done this computer trick. How could they possibly have?"

Donovan shrugged angrily. "Any number of ways, I suppose. There's talk of bandit programs that take over computers. More realistically, there's talk of disappearing programs, that automatically wipe themselves after a certain time—that is, they contain instructions that cause the computer to wipe them, do you see?"

Derec nodded, a memory clicking into place. He'd heard of such programs as toys, but a good computer could usually retain them. And a network of computers... if you were getting food or lodging with your ration tag, that allocation would have to be routed through so many computers that though the *first* computer might lose the program, the memory of the transaction would remain. His little erasure at the hospital had been simple, and he'd caught the accounting trail early, so there was no trace.

But of course there was no memory of their arrival in any Earthly computer. Only in one Earthly positronic brain.

"Violation of the Immigration Act can be charged against you," said Donovan chattily. "We couldn't make it stick without proof that you knowingly and deliberately invaded without the legal formalities. But we could hold you pending an investigation."

"We couldn't go far in any case," said Derec. "Earth is one big jail."

Donovan nodded. "Any planet is."

Derec tried to imagine how many computers in how many bureaus and branches of government would have to be foxed to slip a spy in. His mind boggled; no wonder they were concerned. Far easier to believe that a ship sneaked in and dropped someone, despite orbital radar and other detection devices.

They were overreacting: easier to slip in spies in other guises, like traveling sociology students. Except that Spacers never went anywhere on Earth, and now here were two of them.

"How many of you are there, on Earth?" Donovan asked casually.

It hit Derec that he didn't really know. He had supposed that Dr. Avery worked alone, but his belief that it was so didn't make it so. Besides, Dr. Avery worked through robots, and there could be any number of them—

"I don't know," he said frankly. "We were told little. I have reason to think that we are the only two." He shrugged. "It's hard to find volunteers for social studies on Earth. Too few Spacers care about the subject in the first place; they'd rather study robotics."

Donovan nodded, sitting leaning slightly toward him, not at all relaxed. There was so much energy and sheer *competence* in that pose that Derec had the sudden realization that if he were to attack the Earthman, the other would pinion him as efficiently as any robot. If not quite as gently. The idea of concealing the location of R. David and the apartment seemed silly. This man represented a planetwide investigative organization.

"Most of their agents are robots," he said, and that got an instant response, instantly blanked.

A nice fat red herring for you to follow, he thought gleefully, and then idly wondered what a red herring was, and on what planet the phrase had originated.

"Any idea who *they* are?" Donovan asked, casual again.

Very little. "Only that it's a sociological investigation. There's been some talk about Laws of Humanics, the mathematical expressions that describe how human beings relate to each other. Studies of society have been made on various Spacer worlds, as disparate as Aurora and Solaria." Derec was detailing the theories of certain of the robots of Robot City.

He finished with a shrug. "I suppose that they find Earth the best case study, it having the densest population and the longest cultural history."

"It seemes odd that they'd memory-wipe their agents just for a cultural study," said Donovan dubiously. "What were you instructed to look for?"

Derec thought fast, holding his face as nearly expressionless as he could. He felt that he was sweating. *Keep it close to the truth,* he told himself. "The study's not so important, but uncontaminated data is. If we entered openly, we'd be under the surveillance of your Bureau. Understandable enough; Spacers aren't common on Earth."

"Especially not in the Cities," said Donovan dryly.

"The knowledge that we were being watched, followed, even protected, would affect what we observed. It would be an emotional wall between us and Earth people. It would be a safety net. It would prevent us from living like Earthers."

"And that's what you were sent here to do?" The TBI man was skeptical, but not closed-minded.

"Yes. We weren't told to look for anything specific; that would have warped our data. We were simply told to go to St. Louis, to settle in, to spend some time, and to record our impressions." The moment he spoke the last four words Derec realized how big an error he'd made.

Then he thought of an explanation. But he was still sweating when the Terry said, "But that doesn't explain why your memories were erased."

"Oh. To prevent us from telling anything about the techniques by which our IDs were wiped from your computers. You see, they wanted us to disappear completely, to prevent contamination."

Donovan nodded slowly. Derec couldn't tell how much of it he had swallowed.

"I see. Well, you have not yourself violated any law that we know of, except as accessory to violation of the Immigration Act, and computer fraud. The last of which can't be proven, because we have no records to cite! We've found platinum and iridium that we think must have been dumped by your organization to pay for your support here. There's also some hafnium we can't trace a source for. You, or they, have more than paid for all you've consumed, so there are no complaints on that score."

Donovan looked severely at him. "You understand that there are a lot of red faces at the TBI, and some angry ones elsewhere in Washington. I'm just the A-in-C of the local office, and even I felt the heat. They don't, we don't, like having our computers messed with so freely, gato. But nobody wants trouble either—certainly we don't want to see you lynched. Sorry about your wife. Hope she gets better. We suggest that you leave as soon after that as possible."

Derec nodded, gulping, glad the other didn't ask to see the "impressions" they were supposedly recording. He could say she'd been taken sick so rapidly they hadn't had time—true enough, too. Leaving when Ariel got better was a good idea, too—and not just because of the sternly repressed dislike on the special agent's face.

Ater that, things got worse. For five days in a row they refused to let Derec see Ariel. Afterward, he could see her, but only her trimensional image; he wasn't allowed in the room. She passed through the crisis of the disease during that time, and they began to implant the earliest memories. That left her in an hypnotic state most of the time, and when she wasn't in it she was asleep or on the verge of sleep.

"Somnambulistic state," Dr. Powell said. "Though of course she can't walk. Too weak yet."

Derec grimly worked at recording and coding, eating little and sleeping less. Dreams of Robot City haunted him waking and sleeping. He couldn't help brooding, while working, over such nonsensical questions as: did Dr. Avery get out of Robot City before it was shrunk, or was a tiny madman swimming through his bloodstream at this moment?

How about the Human Medical Team; were they making the most of their opportunity to study human anatomy and biochemistry?

Earthers whom he passed in the corridors and ways tended to avoid him; he looked sick and desperate, as his infrequent glances in mirrors told him. Not all Earthers avoided him, however. Once a man glanced directly at him in Personal, and Derec was so accustomed to Earthly ways that he was shocked. Then he thought for a startled moment that it was Donovan. But it wasn't the special agent, it was merely a man who looked like him: a man with an easy, athletic carriage, an air of competence, and the look of eagles in his eyes.

Another such man sat across from him at breakfast one morning, and occasionally he was half-conscious of other TBI men about. Nothing so conspicuous as ducking into corners as he came by, or peering from doorways. They simply were about.

He decided not to worry about it. The Terries had compelling reasons of their own for not making a scene, and so long as he gave no evidence of spying, he doubted they'd do anything. Probably they were there for *his* protection. Derec grinned faintly, the only hint of humor in all that bleak time: they were contaminating his observations.

"I told you so," he said to the absent Donovan.

Being watched by the TBI did not bother him; he was used to being watched by mother-hen robots.

He did think much, though, on what the Terry had told him: he had never had the plague, though he had antitoxins to its neurotoxin in his blood. He'd had the memory loss without the plague. He'd received a dose of the neurotoxin without having had the disease.

Well, his arrival on that ice asteroid, without his memory, while the robots were searching for the Key to Perihelion, never had seemed to him like an accident or a coincidence. He felt, and always had, as if he were a piece in a game, being herded across the board for someone else's reasons. A mad someone else.

The only one he knew of with both the madness and the genius was Dr. Avery.

They had to get back to Robot City.

One morning during this period he looked up from table J-9 and saw Korolenko next to him. She was wearing her hospital whites, or he might not have recognized her.

"Eat your bacon," she said crisply as recognition dawned on his face.

The thought made him ill. Yeast-based or no, it was fat and greasy and sickening. His opinion of the bacon showed on his face.

"Then eat the eggs. And the toast." Korolenko's voice was grim. "Look, Mr. Avery, you won't help your wife by collapsing of starvation."

Derec wanted to say it was stress, not starvation, but realized that there was something in what she said. He'd been living on fruit juices and caffeine. He managed to choke down the toast and some of the scrambled eggs, with lots of hot, sweet tea.

"That's better. We'll see you at the hospital tomorrow."

That night Derec had one of his worst dreams about Robot City, and the next day he sat looking at nothing and thinking about it.

Nothing silly about Dr. Avery shrinking, or the Human Medical Team. He knew perfectly well that Robot City was on its own planet—even during the dream. What he was dreaming was that a miniature version had been injected into his blood, where it had started growing and reproducing. Here the dream became silly—the miniature city was getting iron from his red blood cells. But there was nothing silly about the feeling it left him with.

Come to think of it, Robot City could be thought of as a kind of infection of the planet on which it had been established. It, too, had grown from a single point of infection, a living organism that had grown and reproduced.

Robot City inside him. He could feel it there. The feeling was so strong that he forgot all about eating, or going to the hospital. Even Ariel was faint in the back of his mind.

Ariel awoke slowly, stretched tired limbs, and looked about. The hospital. It seemed to stretch into the remote past. She could scarcely remember a time when it wasn't all around her. The world beyond it was vague in her mind. A city, she recalled. No, a City, a City of Earth, a humming hive of people, people, people. Beyond, though, was space, and stars, and the Spacer worlds.

Robot City was there, and Derec, and the Human Medical Team. Wolruf and Mandelbrot, who had been called Alpha, long ago. Aranimas, too, was out there somewhere. Beyond that—Aurora. She couldn't remember. Aurora—everybody knew about Aurora. Planet of the Dawn, first settled from Earth, land of peace and contentment and civilization, richest and most powerful of the Spacer worlds.

The world she had called home, and which had exiled her, leaving her to die alone.

But no memories came.

She couldn't remember her homeworld. She couldn't remember her parents, her school, her first robot.

Of course not. She had had amnemonic plague—Burundi's fever, they called it in the Spacer worlds. She had lost her memory.

But she was alive. Ariel began to weep.

A robot was at her bedside, a silly Earth robot with a cheerful face. "Mrs. Avery, are you well? We have been ordered to minimize drug dosages to let you recuperate, but if your distress is too intense we can give you tranquilizers."

With an effort, she calmed herself enough to say, "Thank you, but I am quite well. I merely weep in relief that I am alive. I did not expect to survive."

The spell broken, she found the weeping fit over. She was hungry. She told them so, and was promptly fed. Afterward, feeling tired, very tired, vastly tired, from long lying in even the cleverest hospital bed with all its muscle tone-retaining tricks, she drifted off to sleep.

When Ariel awoke, she was aware again of who she was and that she had had amnemonic plague. She had survived! They told her that her memories would return gradually, based on the foundation they had implanted in her brain. She didn't believe them, but she didn't care. She was alive!

When she had eaten again, they told her, "Your husband is here."

Husband! For an awful moment she was totally blank. "My what?"

They led in a thin, hollow-eyed boy.

"Your husband—Derec Avery," said the robot.

After a moment, she recognized—

"His name isn't Derec!" she said, and at his anguished expression she halted. No—David was dead, he had died of carbon monoxide poisoning on Robot City. No—he had disappeared—she didn't know what had happened—her memories were scrambled, or gone.

Derec!

After a moment she asked, hesitantly, half knowing it was wrong, half fearing it was wrong, "Husband?"

"Why, of course," said he, smiling. He looked so thin, the smile was a grimace on his wasted cheeks. Her heart bumped painfully, and she felt a pricking in her eyes. One of his eyes closed and opened as he continued confidently, "Some things come back faster than others, they tell me— not much of a compliment to me that our wedding wasn't the *first* thing you remembered!"

Ariel smiled and thought: *Avery!* She couldn't remember how that name of all names was stuck on them—she knew *he* hadn't been going under it. But no doubt there was a logical explanation that she would remember in due time. She remembered now their escape from Robot City, their use of the Key, leaving Wolruf and Mandelbrot, and their arrival on Earth in a sparse apartment.

Still smiling faintly, she leaned back and said, "I do remember now, but it's all a little faint—like, like a remembered dream. I hope you won't quiz me on it till I've had time to remember more."

"Of course not," he said, and the instant he had completed the phrase, a robot broke in.

"The doctors' directions are that you not attempt to force the memories. It would be better, Mr. Avery, if you never questioned her about your past or hers."

"Yes, I've been told. Thank you," he said, with true Spacer politeness toward robots. Here in the hospital, the medtechs and nurses called them all *boy!*

"So when can I get out of this place and—and *out?*" she asked, feeling the suffocating terror of claustrophobia closing in. Gamely, she fought against it. It had been her constant companion since arriving in the hospital, and all during her illness she had battled it. If not for tranquilizers, she'd have lost her mind while losing her memory.

"Well, you're still pretty weak physically, and the doctors are not sure yet about your memory. They want to keep you here for a couple more days just on mind games. After that —I dunno. R. Jennie, do you know?"

"Mrs. Avery must have several days of physical therapy before she can safely leave the hospital, Mr. Avery," said the robot. "As for her memory, and her mind generally, I have not been informed."

"If I don't get out of here soon, I'll go mad!" she said with a sudden vehemence that startled her. There was an impulse to resist what her conditioning told her was a lapse into madness, but she had had all she could take of concrete caverns and crowds of—of troglodytes. "I want to see the sun again, and breathe air, and—and feel the grass, and—"

Abruptly she was weeping, for in the midst of this catalog of sights that she had not seen since her memory began, there came a sudden demanding vision: an image of a garden, somewhere, of bright light and flowers and warmth, drowsy warmth, with bees humming sweetly on key, and the scent of orange blossoms. Someone she loved lay just out of sight.

Ariel turned over and wept passionately for some minutes, her face in her pillow. She felt a hand on her shoulder, not a robotic hand, and felt faintly grateful, but was too wretched to turn.

A detached, floating calm gradually washed away her tears, leaving her tired but spent. Tranquilizer; the robots never gave her more than a few minutes to weep. They usually allowed her that—or she'd have gone mad from the inability to express her emotions at all.

When she turned, Korolenko was there, frowning in conversation with—Derec, she must remember always to call him. That was right, that was what the Earthers called him. But there was another reason, which she couldn't quite recall, why she must not use his true name. Or did she know his true name, after all? She had forgotten so much, could she trust that memory too?

Avery! she thought, remotely astonished. The drug made all emotions remote.

She wondered vaguely where Dr. Avery was now. Still on Robot City, she supposed. For a moment she felt an ironic amusement at the thought that they had been using his apartment, his robot, and his funds on Earth. Then she knew that this was an old amusement, she'd had this thought before; and with that thought, she remembered having had the amusement before.

"Memory is like drink," she said to the uncomprehending robot. She felt a little light-headed.

The nurse and a robot stepped aside as they spoke together and Ariel looked, shocked, at . . . Derec.

"Why is . . . he so—thin?" she demanded abruptly.

"Mr. Avery? He had been under a strain, Mrs. Avery. He

has been worried about you and has not been eating sufficiently."

"Does he have—" Her heart stopped, started painfully.
"—Burundi's fever?" Again her heart shook her.

"No, Mrs. Avery. He is merely under a strain."

"He's sick," she said.

"No, Mrs. Avery."

"He is sick," Ariel said positively, peering at him nar-
rowly with the observant eyes of one who has recently
passed near to the gates of death. "He is—dying."

Nurse Korolenko heard enough of that to frown at her,
and one of the robots—R. Jennie, Ariel thought—went to
the control board at the head of the bed, but merely checked
the readings.

"Derec is a young fool who has neither been sleeping nor
eating, and who has spent all his time brooding over you,"
said Korolenko, angry not at her or at Derec, but at his
stupidity.

"There's nothing else to do in that stupid apartment but
stare at the ceiling," Ariel said, irritated on his behalf. Why
did he keep staring at her with eyes like holes in space?
"Frost, there's not even a trimensional there."

"You wanted to experience life as Earth people do, and
apparently low-rated Earth people at that, so you have no
more than they do," Korolenko said, shrugging.

Wanted . . . to experience . . . ? She turned eyes in inquiry
on . . . Derec, who shrugged also, grimacing ruefully.

"Perhaps you don't remember that the Institute wiped our
memories temporarily before we came to Earth, so we
wouldn't be able to reveal their techniques," he said.

Ariel could only stare in amazement.

"When you are well enough to travel, we will leave. Of
course, since we've been discovered here, our purpose of
sociological study is negated. And once back on Aurora, we
will have our own recorded memories reimplanted."

She had heard of none of this. The Institute? Institute of
what? Study? Of *Earth?* But, *own recorded memories
reimplanted. . . .* Ariel leaned back and for a moment

thought tears would leak from her eyes.

"So you've lost your memory twice over, but it's only temporary."

"I'd like to know just how that's done," growled a baritone voice. After a moment Ariel identified it: Dr. Powell. She had heard it often enough in the past weeks. "I know, I know, you haven't the foggiest—only a brief layman's description that doesn't describe."

When she opened her eyes, they were all around her bed, with R. Jennie at the controls.

"Well, young lady, your request for a visit to the outdoors is a bit . . . unusual." He visibly repressed a shudder of distaste at the thought, and Ariel, fascinated, realized that to this man the outside was more fear-inspiring than the claustrophobic City was to her.

"We can't very well add you to the list on a Settler Acclimatization Group, and the only other people who go . . . outside are the odd Farming, Mining, and Pelagic Overseers. They are solitary as well as agoraphilic, very strange types; they wouldn't welcome an addition. Certainly not a sick Spacer. And there's nobody else to take care of you."

"Robots?" she asked weakly, looking at R. Jennie.

The doctor frowned, shook his head. "It's difficult to move a robot through the City without having it mobbed and destroyed. Robots are being restricted more and more each year; we have half as many here now at Towner Laney than when I was an intern. That leaves only your husband, and frankly, within a couple of days you'll be taking care of him."

"I'm all right," said Derec with a flash of irritation that for a moment brought back the companion of the hospital station—Ariel couldn't remember the name, but she remembered the station—and of Robot City. "What's the signal coding of the local office of the TBI?"

"The what?" Dr. Powell stared at him. "The comm number? Why would you want to call the Terries?" From his tone it was obvious he had guessed, and seethed at the thought.

"To get authorization to have robots moved through the motorways, and for permission to leave the City, if only for a short period."

"Hmmph! Medically—"

"Medically it would do her good, Doctor," said the nurse quietly.

"True, damn it, but we need to be sure that her mental condition—the implants—"

"We can't keep bringing her back and forth, I admit," said Korolenko.

"Ariel, could you...hold off till tomorrow?" Derec asked.

Tomorrow...she was so tired, from inaction and drugs, that she'd sleep till then anyway...Ariel could have stood anything for a tomorrow in the sun.

"Oh, yes, yes." She'd be good, she'd—

Ariel had a moment of vivid memory, herself quite young, promising her mother that she would be very, very good. Was that when she'd been given her first robot? Or was that Boopsie, the pup?

When the first vivid reexperience faded, she looked up and they had drawn apart. It was no matter; it would be all right tomorrow.

"Never saw myself as nursemaid to a couple of Spacers and a robot," said Donovan. The agent-in-charge had not trusted any of his men to go outside.

The hospital had an emergency entrance and egress for ambulances, and was a major junction on the motorways. R. Jennie carried Ariel down in its arms, Ariel having chosen that over being wheeled, strapped to a gurney, or in a chair with wheels.

The hospital had supplied an ambulance, but the Terry eyed it with distaste. "We'll use the Bureau car," he said. "There's room for four of us, robot or no."

R. Jennie gently put Ariel into the back seat and got in beside her, the car creaking and sinking under the weight until the suspension system analyzed the imbalance and compensated for it. Derec and Donovan got into the front seat, and the agent took the controls and sent them surging silently down a ramp and into a lit but dim-seeming tunnel.

For a moment Ariel fought a scream, tensing; the claustrophobia was worse in such tight passages. But she fought it off, helped by the speed of their passage. Signs blurred past soundlessly as the Terry tapped more and more of the beamed power. Once the ceiling lit up in bloody light, and winking yellow arrows along the walls gave obscure warning. Then a blue car whipped by in the other direction, Donovan having avoided it with the warning.

"Like the models we trained on," murmured Derec, glancing back at her.

For a moment she was blank on that, the she remembered the roofless roads and the emergency vehicle monitors, the remote control sweaty in her hand, and the laughing students crowding around. But that was nothing like this dim, empty wormhole.

GLENDALE, KIRKWOOD, MANCHESTER, WINCHESTER, BALLWIN, ELLISVILLE, the signs flowed past, as fast as the expressway would have taken them. Ariel ignored all the labyrinthine branchings and windings that twisted obscurely away right and left out of sight, peering past Derec to see as far before them as possible.

The tunnel was a rectangle of dim light, two glowing tracks overhead and a pair of glowing, beaded tracks on the sides, the last being the glowing signs, fading into tininess.

At last, though, there came an interruption in the shape of the tunnel. It got dark at the limit of vision, the darkness outlined in light. Presently the outline of light appeared as various warning signs. The darkness was a ramp, leading up.

Donovan slowed sharply, causing R. Jennie to lean forward and prepare itself for a snatch at the controls.

"Don't worry, boy," said the Terry, grinning but not look-ing back. Ariel had him in profile. "I've driven for thou-sands of hours, faster than this, and no problems."

"Twenty-one point three percent of all major traumas to enter Towner Laney Memorial Hospital occur in the motor-ways," said R. Jennie, unperturbed. "Fewer than twenty percent occur on the ways. A few thousand humans use the motorways; seven million use the ways."

"Damn, I always hated know-it-all robots," grunted Don-ovan, taking the ramp with unnecessary flair. "Could never stand to live on any Spacer world. A man should have the right to go to hell in his own way."

The car eased to a stop at a barrier. Donovan played a tune on his computer controls and the barrier opened. He drove through, they wound a complicated path that appar-ently avoided heavy traffic—there were thunderous rushing sounds through the walls, but no traffic in their motorway—and they were at a huge entry in the outer wall.

Kilometer-long lines of great trucks full of produce, some robot-driven, most computer-controlled, roared in with noisy, huge tires but silent engines and dived into the City just below them. They were on a higher ramp, one of a dozen that leaped out of the City from high and low. Dono-van stopped the car well back from that light-blazing gap.

"You'll have to walk from here," he said abruptly. "Car won't go any further—no beameast beyond the barrier."

CHAPTER 13
ROBOT CITY AGAIN

"Paulins," said R. Jennie. "They are used to cover machinery in the fields against rain and dew. There are no tents available in the immediate vicinity of St. Louis. Perhaps in a day or two there will be a tent."

The plasticated canvas of the big paulins worked as well as a tent, strung over a couple of poles and tied to a tree limb. It was needed more for shade than shelter. This move to the country had not been a simple one, nor could they keep it up for more than a day or two.

But it was such a relief!

Ariel could tell that Derec felt the same sense of escape that she did. The sky of Earth was wide and blue and very high, and little puffy clouds ambled slowly across it, all framed by the pointed opening of the "tent." The sunlight was just right. The plants were the familiar green of Earth life everywhere, and they too seemed just right. Except in greenhouses, she had probably never seen Earthly plants in the natural light of the sun in which they evolved. Even the heat was not unpleasant.

"We won't need a tent, if we have to wait that long," said Derec grimly.

"You should return to the City as soon as you can," R. Jennie said. "Mrs. Avery is far from recovered from the fever."

Ariel felt quite recovered from the fever, though her memory was returning slowly. Weak as she undoubtedly was, she thought with concern, she could have wrestled Derec two falls out of three and won. But he said nothing about his own condition.

"Everything's so . . . ordinary," said Ariel, looking out at the kind of birds and plants and small animals she had seen all her life. A squirrel is a squirrel, and sounds just the same on Aurora. Even the shrilling of the unseen insects was familiar. Humans had taken their familiar symbiotic life-forms with them to the stars. She had expected Earth to be more exotic.

The reality was a relief more than a disappointment.

"It must have been a bad time for you," she said to Derec, when R. Jennie had stepped out to the . . . kitchen. They had been supplied with something called a "hot plate" and a dielectric oven.

Derec moodily watched the robot prepare the packaged meals, designed for people with high enough ratings to permit them to eat in their own apartments. This was luxury for their rate.

"Bad, well." He shrugged, clearly not wishing to discuss it. "I did learn one thing from R. David: there's a spaceship belonging to Dr. Avery in the New York port. If we could get there—"

"How, if our rating doesn't permit us to travel that far?"

"We'll have to get him to make ID with higher ratings for us—"

R. Jennie stepped under the opening with a tray holding coffee and juices. When she had gone, Ariel said, "I hope they don't discover the apartment."

"I suspect the Terries know all about it, but won't make trouble. They want us gone before we get mobbed or something. We've been very lucky."

"Couldn't we ask Donovan for assistance?" she asked wistfully.

"We could. I thought of it," Derec said, broodingly. "But that'd be above his level, surely. If Earth can ignore us, it won't be so badly embarrassed if we're discovered here, investigating—or spying on—Earth people. But if they have helped us in any way, they can't deny having known about us."

"Helping us would be seen as condoning our presence," she said grayly. "I understand." Politics seemed to be the same everywhere. "So what can we do? Get new ID—will the Terries spot that, do you think?"

"Frost, I don't know—"

R. Jennie gave them fruit cups and whipped cream, returned to the kitchen, a rustic scene in the frame of the tent opening.

The fruit was good, but unusual—compotes served in what she thought of as unsweetened ice cream cones. It was like eating warm ice cream with strong fruit flavors. All yeast, she supposed.

"If they do spot us at it, I suppose they'd look the other way. But what worries me is that it would alarm them. They'd know we weren't telling everything, they'd realize that R. David—or someone—has ID duplicating equipment. They might well raid the apartment."

Ariel thought about that for a moment. As long as they weren't arrested and the Key to Perihelion taken from them, it didn't matter.

"Oh. The Key is focused on the apartment," she said. "We'd be unable to retreat to it." She remembered well the occasion when they'd had to do so.

"We will be in any case; we couldn't begin to explain our reappearance," Derec said. "They'd guess too much—"

"Zymoveal," said R. Jennie. "There is also a chicken wing for each of you. Chicken soup, made of real chicken with yeast enhancement. Bread, real potatoes, gravy."

A simple, hearty meal. Ariel ate with good appetite, but her stomach seemed to have shrunk. Weeks of eating little in hospital had altered her eating habits. Derec, however, carried on grimly, eating long after it became obvious that he'd had all he wanted, eating on to the edge of nausea.

When the robot had retreated, Ariel said, "I see. It's all or nothing. Well, if so I won't weep. If we could just get to New York!"

"Don't think I haven't thought about it. I'd be tempted to walk—it's on this continent—but it's a couple of thousand kilometers, and we'd starve."

"Too bad. Derec, why do you go on eating when anyone can see you're full?"

He looked up at her grimly, harassed, his eyes sunken, his face thin and lined. "I've not been eating enough, or sleeping well enough. Everybody says so. I need to get my strength back now that you're well."

"Have you really worried that much about me?" she asked, her heart thumping. She felt flattered, and also dismayed, as if it were her fault.

"Well, it isn't just that." Derec lowered his fork, swallowed coffee, looked queasy. "I've been upset. I haven't been sleeping. I-I keep having this strange stupid dream. About Robot City."

Ariel stared at him. "A stupid dream made you look like a walking wreck?"

"Yes." He looked . . . frightened. "Ariel, there's something unusual about this. I-I keep dreaming that Robot City is *inside* me. We've got to get back there."

Robot City!

Ariel's mind was flooded with a hundred images, sounds, odors even, of the great robot-inhabited planet, where the busy machines worked away like so many bees, building and building for the ultimate good of humans. It was an Earthly City without a roof, populated by robots rather than humans. They'd been trapped there, first by the robots themselves, then by their mad designer, Dr. Avery.

"Go back there?" she whispered tensely. "I'll never go back!"

"We must," said Derec, his voice just as low and determined, but also indifferent. It was as if he was speaking not to her but to himself. "I'm dying or something. I don't know what Dr. Avery did to me, but . . ."

What had he not already done? Derec had lost his memory long ago, and only Dr. Avery could have removed it. She had known that as soon as she realized that he had lost all memory of her. Human beings were less than robots to Avery, they were guinea pigs.

Go back? To save Derec's life?

But I'm cured! she wanted to cry. I can go back to Aurora and say to them: Look, the despised Earthers cured me after you cast me out! You don't need to watch your sons and daughters lose their memories and die—you can cure them. If you can persuade the Earthers to tell you how!

There need be no more of this aimless existence, running from planet to planet, looking for a cure, for an excuse to go on hoping. There could be a home, a place in society, all the wealth of associations that membership in the human society meant.

They could even consider the Keys, the existence of aliens, Robot City itself—they could report Dr. Avery, turn the Key over to the proper authority, shift the burden to other shoulders.

Ariel sighed.

"You don't look good," she said.

After all, how much did she owe him, anyway? At lot of apologies, if nothing else. She'd blamed him wrongly for too much.

"I hope there are star charts in the ship," he said. Derec put a hand to his brow. "If we can get back to Kappa Whale, we can take both ships back to Robot City. That'll give us a spare. Dr. Avery won't think of that—I hope." He rubbed his face slowly; his eyes squinted as if the light were too bright.

"Is it getting dark?" he asked.

"Not yet," Ariel said. "The sun will be setting in a little while, but it won't start to get dark for another hour."

"Oh."

"What kind of dreams have you been having?" she asked skeptically, thinking that they might have been right: if he'd not been eating or sleeping, it might all be strain—

"Like I said, I dream that Robot City has been shrunk into my bloodstream. I don't know why it frosts me so, but it does. I can't shake it off. It's a —a *haunting* feeling." He rubbed his face again, haggard.

Ariel didn't know what to say. "It . . . doesn't sound like an ordinary dream."

"I'm sure it's no dream," he said instantly, looking sick. "Something's going on." R. Jennie entered the opening of the tent and he said, dully, "R. Jennie, what are chemfets?"

"I do not know, Mr. Avery."

"Derec—"

"I wish I could sleep. It drives you crazy if you don't have real dreams."

"Derec, you really look—awful." Ariel felt a stab of real fear. "Oh, Derec!"

He looked as if he were about to throw up. Drooling, he pushed his light camp chair back, starting to get up. He fell over.

"Derec!"

R. Jennie came with a rush, cradled him as Derec's arms and legs started to flail. "He is having convulsions. I do not know what is wrong," she said. "Help me hold him—"

Ariel was too weak herself to be of much help, but after a few moments Derec's seizure eased, he sighed heavily, and he began to breathe in a more normal fashion instead of inhaling in great tortured gasps. His limbs relaxed, and R. Jennie warily lowered him to the carpet-covered grass of the tent floor.

"He seems to be much better, but this is not a natural sleep," said the robot. "Unfortunately, there is no communo in the area, nor do I possess a subetheric link. I must go for help. Ariel, you must watch him."

"What do I do if he . . . has another seizure?" she asked, huskily.

"Hold him. Do not put a spoon in his mouth." And with that puzzling admonition, the robot began to run toward the City.

Greatly to her relief, Derec awoke within ten minutes.

"How are you?" she whispered, frightened.

"I'm okay," he said faintly. He did look greatly relieved. "Chemfets," he said.

"What?"

"Robot City *is* inside me, in a manner of speaking." Derec struggled with her weak help to a sitting position. "I'm thirsty."

Hastily, Ariel poured him some juice. He drank carefully, seeming a little dizzy.

"We keep thinking of robots in terms of positronic brains," he said, seemingly at random. "But computers existed before positronic brains and are still widely in use. At least a dozen computers of different sizes for every positronic brain, even on the Spacer worlds. And for a long time there've been desultory attempts to reduce computers in size and give them some of the characteristics of life."

"Derec—are you all right?"

He looked at her seriously, haunting knowledge in his sunken eyes. "No. I've been infected with chemfets. Microscopic, self-replicating computer circuits. Robot City *is* in my bloodstream. When I fell asleep just now, the monitor that Dr. Avery implanted in my brain opened communication with them."

"What . . . what are they doing?" Ariel could scarcely grasp it, it was so strange. What would a chemfet want? Was it truly alive?

"Growing and multiplying, at the moment. I don't think they're anywhere near . . . call it maturity. The monitor . . . I don't think it's of any use yet. It's as if they have nothing to say to me yet."

"But they may later?" she asked swiftly.

"I suppose." He looked at her, haggard. "I wonder if they've been programmed with the Three Laws?"

Ariel grunted. "Yes. I suppose they've been upsetting your body systems. No wonder you've been sick. Will . . . will the dreams continue?"

He thought about it, shook his head. "I don't think so. I think those were just the monitor trying to open contact.

Once the channel is opened, it won't be worked unless they have something to say."

"How about if you have something to say to them?" Ariel asked, with a flash of anger.

"I suppose . . . if I learn how to work the monitor," he said dubiously.

"And tell them to get out of your body because they're killing you! First Law," she said.

Then: "I *hope* they're programmed with the Three Laws." Frightened, she looked at him.

Strength and purpose seemed to have flowed back into him: knowledge of what was going on, a drop in the subtle pressure the monitor had been putting on him, relief, a good meal. It was something merely to know what the problem was.

"We've got to get back to Robot City," he said with determination. "I now know that part of my feeling on that was due to the pressure of the monitor. The chemfets want me back there for some reason. But we have our own reason for going back. We've got to confront Dr. Avery and make him reverse this—infestation."

Ariel nodded in angry agreement. "Yes! Dr. Avery has played his games with us, and especially with you, for too long."

He stood up, and though he leaned on the table, he seemed much stronger. "But how do we get off Earth?"

"We'll have to consult with R. David. If we can get back to the apartment without a lot of . . ."

"Where's R. Jennie?"

"She's gone for help. You had—convulsions."

"No wonder my muscles are sore. She's gone for—doctors? I can't let them examine me—"

Ariel grunted in understanding. "We'd never get away— they'd hospitalize you." She looked at him. "They might even be able to cure you."

Derec said, "I've come to have a lot of respect for Earth's doctors, but this is a matter of robotics. I think we'd better go back to the source. I'd like to know what reason Dr.

Avery had for this—what did he hope to accomplish?"

Ariel could only shake her head. "Just using you as a guinea pig, I suppose."

"Yes, but that shows that he has some reason for developing chemfets, even if he doesn't care about me. There must be some use for them." As he spoke, Derec was groping in his pockets. He produced the Key to Perihelion. "At least, with R. Jennie gone, we can vanish without any questions being asked."

"Questions will be asked," she warned him.

"Yes," Derec said, pressing the corners and taking her hand. "But not of us."

Perihelion's gray nothingness surrounded them. "They'll assume some sensible explanation, involving the imaginary institute that sent us to Earth," Derec added, looking around in the gray fog.

"I guess so," she said dubiously. "As long as we aren't spotted in the City."

"Or any other City."

The apartment appeared around them, and Derec sagged with the return to gravity. Alarmed, Ariel threw her arm around him and instantly R. David was there, supporting him from the other side.

"Mr. Avery! What is the matter?"

Derec obviously hadn't prepared an answer.

"Derec is sick," said Ariel swiftly. "We must get him to Aurora for treatment. The spaceship is at New York City Port. How can we get there the soonest?"

"The fastest means of travel on Earth is by air," said R. David. The robot hesitated, bending over to assure itself that Derec wasn't dying at that moment.

"I'll be okay," said Derec, his voice low but firm.

"What's the fastest means of travel that our rating will permit us to use?" Ariel asked.

"Air travel," said the robot.

"Isn't it rationed?"

"No," said the robot. "You see, on Earth, necessities are

rationed on an as-needed basis. Scarce luxuries, such as real meat and fish, or larger and better quarters, are rationed mostly on a basis of social standing. Some of the less-scarce luxuries, such as candy and birthday cards, are available partly on a rationing basis and partly on a cash basis. These are the so-called 'discretionary luxuries,' minor items not everyone wants.

"Finally, luxuries in large supply are distributed purely on a monetary basis, and this includes air travel. The air system was designed for emergencies. Since Earth people hate to travel by air, the excess is freely available. It is expensive, but your bank account cards are amply charged."

Ariel fumbled through her wallet for the window with the cash card. Was it a real memory, or did she dream that she had dropped her purse on the expressway? A dream; or else R. David had replaced the ID. "Will our use of cash be monitored?" she asked.

"That is not possible. The privacy laws of Earth forbid scrutiny or oversight of these monetary transfers, so the provision doesn't exist."

Since money could only be used for "minor luxuries," no wonder. "How do we get to an airport?"

R. David gave minute directions for taking the expressway to something he called Lambert Field, and after Derec had rested for a few minutes they went out to the communo and called for reservations on the next flight to New York. After two hours of fearful waiting for the knock of the TBI on the door, they ventured out for what Ariel devoutly hoped would be the last time through the corridors and ways of the City.

Each step of that passage brought back memories from just before the crisis of the amnemonic plague. This time they rode the way only to the north-south junction, changed ways, and rode north for longer than they had ridden east on their previous excursion: BRENTWOOD, RICHMOND HEIGHTS, CLAYTON, UNIVERSITY CITY, VINITA PARK, CHARLACK, the forgotten political divisions of a simpler time. ST. JOHN, COOL VALLEY, KINLOCH.

And then, after thirty minutes of standing and holding on, fearing every moment that Derec would collapse, they saw LAMBERT FIELD AIRPORT, EXIT LEFT.

The airport was a sleepy place, considering St. Louis City's seven million people. There was but one ticket window, the clerk there seemed subdued, and the few people in the waiting rooms never spoke or smiled. Presently their plane was announced.

Not only was the passage to the place covered, but the *runway* it took off from was also roofed over! There were no windows in the place, so they had a choice of sleeping or of watching the continuous news and entertainment feed in front of each seat. Earthers scheduled most flights for night, and the five other passengers—only five! Ariel remembered the crowded millions on the ways—the other passengers elected to sleep, those who could. Most were too nervous to try. Derec slept all the way to New York, to Ariel's intense satisfaction. She slept most of the way herself. Best of all, in the air and the airports, nobody spoke to them or even looked at them.

Derec looked up at the ship in relief and wonder. "I can't believe we made it," he said.

"We haven't gotten in yet," said Ariel, edgily.

He approached and inserted his ID tab into the slot. After a moment, it opened. "Of course," he murmured. "R. David gave us compatible IDs."

The ship was a Star Seeker, identical, or nearly so, to the one they'd left in orbit around Kappa Whale. On the ground, it was clumsy getting around inside it, but that was normal. They climbed slowly to the bow control room.

Ariel climbed easily—like Derec, not pushing it—and he was relieved to see that she was gaining strength day by day. He himself felt better after last night's sleep than he had in weeks, but knew that his reserves were still very low. The acceleration seat was a relief after the climb.

"Checklist, please," he said, depressing the *Ship* key and speaking to the air. The ship obediently displayed a checklist on a visor, and they went over it carefully. Some items had to be checked personally, most importantly, food. Ariel reported with concern that that was a low item.

"Only a few imperishables," she said, "a few packages of radiation-preserved foods and some cans."

Derec hesitated. That could be serious.

"What do you think?"

"I'd say take the chance," Ariel said. "The TBI must be going mad over our disappearance. If they do a computer check, they may wonder about this Spacer ship. Don't tell me they don't watch carefully every takeoff and landing."

Of course they wouldn't be able to interfere; Earthers had little control over their own port, as they owned few ships. Still, if he and Ariel started shopping for food—

"Right. We'll go."

When they requested clearance it was readily given, and Derec primed the jets and goosed the micropile. The tubes burst into muffled thunder. He switched to air-breathing mode as soon as they had a little speed, and took an economical high-G trajectory into space. In minutes, the great blue world was off to one side.

"Which way?" Ariel asked.

There was a slight technical advantage in aiming one's ship toward one's objective, since intrinsic velocity was unaltered by passage through hyperspace. But the adjustment could be made at the other end.

"Straight out," he said. "I'm not exactly afraid of pursuit, but—"

"Right."

"Straight out" was in the direction Earth was traveling. Ariel calculated their fuel and Derec elected to use twenty percent. He liked a lot of maneuvering reserve. The burn wasn't long, and when it was over, Earth had not altered much. It was more aft of them, and only a bit smaller. Now, though, there was a wall of delta-V between them and it: in order to catch them, any ship would have to match their change of velocity—their delta-V.

"We've got time to kill," Derec said, feeling tired. Reaction weighed him down even in the absence of gravity.

"Think we should rig the condenser?" Ariel asked.

The thought of the excursion in a space-suit made him feel even more tired. Then he thought: *Of course, Ariel can do it. She's not sick any more.*

She was still weak, though, despite her rapid recovery. And he himself was not up to it.

"It's only for a week or two," he said. "I think the ship can handle it. It's only for two people, also."

Ariel nodded. "Listen," she said. "How do you feel? You

seem better after your sleep, but you're still sick. Just knowing what's going on inside hasn't cured you."

That was true. "I feel tired at the moment. Why?"

"I want to talk about Robot City. I want to talk to you about everything we went through together, right back to the control room of Aranimas's ship, before Rockliffe Station."

She looked at him, her eyes big and intent. "I want all the help you can give me to recover my memory."

That he could understand. "Of course, I'll be glad to help. I just wish I could be more helpful."

Ariel opened her mouth, closed it, her face pink. "Derec . . ." she said. "I . . . Derec, I'm sorry I didn't tell you more about yourself—about us. But I couldn't! I couldn't tell you I had amnemonic plague. And I-I can't talk about us—from before. I'm not sure of my memories—I've lost so much, and I don't know how much I can trust of what I have now. I'm sorry—but it's just too uncertain—and too painful."

Illness can make a person's mind preternaturally clear. This was a girl who had been exiled and disinherited for having contracted a hideous disease. "Of course."

Her feeling for him was obvious—the attraction, the repulsion, pain and pleasure intertwined in memories he didn't share. Memories that now she couldn't trust.

"No need to apologize," he said gently. "There's been nothing between *us* since Aranimas's control room. Your previous memories, real or unreal, are of a different and forgotten person—whose name I don't even know."

She managed a weak smile. "True, that—person is forgotten. It's true. You are a different person. Derec—do you mind if I don't tell you your—his—name? I'm not sure I really do know it. Besides, it's easier for me to think of you as Derec—"

Derec suppressed a sharp, small pain. His lack of a past was an emptiness that was always with him. "Of course I don't mind," he said. "Some things are more important than others. You are more important to me than any memory."

And that was certainly true.

"Oh, Derec!" Ariel plunged at him, grappled him in a bearhug that sent them wheeling, laughing, through the air of the little ship, colliding with the bulkheads and the control board. Fortunately, the hoods were down over the control sections.

Lingering in the vicinity of Earth for a week was a risky business on several counts, Derec thought, but he had not wanted to burn more fuel unless he had to. Refueling was, in one sense, no problem: the rocket simply heated reaction mass with the micropile and flung it aft at very high velocity. Almost any kind of mass would do, and powdered rock in water—a slurry—was a very good reaction mass. It could be gotten almost anywhere. Water was next best; the ship was equipped to handle slurry, and the pumps could deal easily with water. These items were readily available in space or on planets.

There might not be time to stop and spend ten hours re-fueling, though. And they could well find themselves in a system with abundant fuel for them, but lacking the reserve fuel necessary to maneuver to it.

Ariel was a competent pilot herself, and had been travel-ing on her own for some time—Derec didn't know how long—before being captured by Aranimas. And she was more reckless than he.

"If we're going to spend all this time drifting, why don't we do it in safety—at Kappa Whale? Or off Robot City?"

"If we're pursued, we'll burn more," Derec said. "That would mean we'd have to burn still *more* at Robot City to lose our intrinsic velocity."

"I think we should hurry," she said. "Derec, I'm not happy about your condition. I don't think you're getting bet-ter. Every now and then you go off into a sort of fugue."

It was true that occasionally the monitor opened, and the chemfets festering in his bloodstream droned an emotionless report into his mind about having overcome this or that dif-ficulty or achieved this or that milestone of their growth. He supposed all this would mean much to Dr. Avery. To him it meant nothing, but he was not able to tune out the reports.

"At least I don't go into convulsions anymore," he said. The one incident was all there had been, but Ariel was obviously still frightened by the memory. He was glad he hadn't been able to see himself. "You occasionally have—fugues, I guess, in an even more literal sense—yourself."

She nodded. "I see you do the same thing—I suppose you still have flashes of memory, when memories return, so vividly that you are there."

"Usually when I'm asleep, and I lose most of them," Derec said.

Her memories were returning in a massive way, compared to his own. She wasn't getting anything like a coherent account of her past life, of course, merely a chunk here and a chunk there. Like pages of a book torn out and scattered by the wind, here a leaf caught by a tree, there one against a house.

Four days out from Earth, with the mother planet a mere blue-green brilliant star behind them, now getting closer and closer to Sol, Derec and Ariel agreed that it was safe to open the hyperwave. They called Wolruf and Mandelbrot at Kappa Whale, but got no answer.

"Can you shift the elements so it broadcasts on the same wavelengths as the Keys to Perihelion do?" Ariel asked.

He had told her their deduction about the failure of the hyperwave aboard Dr. Avery's other Star Seeker; she had been in such a feverish state that it hadn't registered with her at the time.

Derec shook his head somberly. "It calls for precision tools and a fairly lengthy research effort. First, just to determine what broadcasts the Keys spray their static on."

"Ship static wavelengths, perhaps?"

"Perhaps. . . . Likely, in fact." Hyperwave static was a fact of life, one the usual hyperwave link was designed to ignore. "But when did you even hear of a hyperlink designed to *pick up* static?"

Ariel smiled faintly, shook her head.

A week out from Earth, they started calculating the Jump to Kappa Whale.

"It hasn't been too long," said Ariel. "Wolruf's food will hold out, of course, and so will their energy. The micropile is good for years yet. They've a sufficient supply of fuel to do what little maneuvering they may require. They could Jump out of Kappa Whale and back to avoid pursuit, if they have to."

"So they should still be there. Where would they go, without us, if they acquired star charts?"

Ariel couldn't guess.

Charts were one of the first things he and Ariel had checked for when they had entered the ship. There was a complete set, and if there hadn't been, they could have requested a copy from Control. One would have been beamed to them immediately, without a question.

"It's easier to calculate a single Jump for Kappa Whale," he said. "But it definitely isn't safer."

Ariel calculated three Jumps, and Derec almost agreed. "The trouble is, Kappa Whale is nearly behind us. Your first Jump turns us in hyper, which is possible, but it's a strain on the engines. I suggest we Jump to Procyon, which is near enough to our line of flight, and do a partial orbit about it, burning to bring us out on direct line for the first of your Jumps."

She bit her lip and said, "I'm sorry. I know I'm too reckless. I think it's because I had a sheltered childhood. I never got hurt much when I was a kid."

Derec grinned. "I have to admit that in my few short months of life I've acquired a healthy respect for the laws of chance."

Their first approximations done, all that remained was to put final figures into the computer and let it solve the equations of the Jump. They needed to know their correct speed and direction with some accuracy, so they would know what to expect when they landed in Procyon's arms.

Ariel bent to the instruments while Derec fumble-fingeredly tried to set up the computer for their first Jump.

After a long time, he said, "Ariel, can you handle this? I can't seem to concentrate, and my fingers are made of rubber."

She looked at him in concern. "I was afraid you were going off into a fever again." Twice before on the trip he had had feverish episodes, as the chemfets altered their growth, in turn altering the environment around them: him.

Derec tried to fight off fear. He had no idea yet of the ultimate purpose of the chemfets, and had not been able to "talk" to them. Worse, he had no idea if he was contagious. After that one hug, they had avoided so much as touching each other, for fear that Ariel, too, would be infected with them.

They could well kill him—and might not care if they did.

"Very well," Ariel said, her voice trembling a little. "Why don't you take some febrifuge and stretch out? Maybe a nap will bring you out of it."

It sounded good to him. The febrifuge had helped break the last fever, they thought. He was swallowing the thick liquid carefully, because of free-fall and a slightly swollen throat, when Ariel cried out.

"Yes?" he said, catching his breath and relieved that he had not choked.

"There's a spaceship closing on us."

Pursuit from Earth? he thought.

The Star Seeker didn't have very good detection apparatus, mostly meteor detection. It was this that had flashed an alarm. Meteors, however, do not move very fast. This object was flashing toward them. The detector gave two readings, and Derec finally—through the throb in his head —concluded that their assailant had come up behind a more slowly moving rock.

"We should be able to get some kind of picture," said Ariel.

"It's still too far off, I think, for a visual image," Derec said. He blinked his eyes to bring his vision back to a single focus. "I wish we had neutrino detectors."

All nuclear power plants gave off neutrinos, and nobody bothers to shield them off. A neutrino reading would give them an estimate of power generating capacity, and thus of ship size. Of course, a battleship and a medium freighter would have similar-sized power plants, but some information would be better than none.

"Heat?"

"It isn't burning at the moment," she told him, consulting the bolometer. "It must have spotted us days ago and burned to intercept."

"Go ahead and enter our Jump in the computer," he said. It was all he could think of, and it wasn't much. "How long will that take?"

"Too long," she said gloomily. "You are right, though. It's the best bet, especially if that's an Earth Patrol ship. Derec, it might follow."

He opened his mouth to say that it didn't matter, then closed it. "Frost!"

They intended to maneuver at Procyon—they might be in the system a week, during which the bigger ship could hunt them down. Nor would there be any hope of help there.

He grasped at a straw. "Bigger ships need more fuel. If he can't match our maneuvers—"

"And you call me reckless. Let's not bet on it, okay?"

"Frost."

The other pilot wasn't maneuvering: he was swooping in to intercept their course from behind and to one side. He'd cross their course at a very sharp angle, pull ahead, and brake down, to let them drift into his arms. He was moving quite rapidly relative to them, far faster than the rock he was coming up behind, and would have to burn soon or swoop helplessly by them.

Their options were limited: they could fire their rockets to speed up, they could roll the ship and burn to slow down, or they could Jump. It would take time to set up the computer for that; Jumping blind might not mean certain death, it might merely mean being permanently lost in the vastness of the galaxy—or the galaxies! In hyper, all parts of the normal universe were equidistant.

Or they could roll the ship ninety degrees and turn aside.

Ariel didn't consider it, and Derec didn't even think of it. They had spent twenty percent of their fuel to acquire their current velocity. They would retain it no matter how much they pushed "sideways" on their course. It would therefore take another twenty percent of their fuel to turn the ship aside at an angle of a mere forty-five degrees—a negligible turn.

"Call for help?" Ariel asked dubiously.

"He'll be on us in twenty minutes or less," said Derec glumly. No help could possibly reach them. "Unless he burns toward us."

"Unlikely."

"True." His head wasn't working right. The rapidly closing ship wouldn't want more velocity toward them; it would have to brake down enough as it was, when it passed.

"I think we can assume that no Earth Patrol will fire on us without sufficient reason," Ariel said. "So I propose that we talk to them as politely as possible, but maintain course and speed. We can burn if necessary, but—"

"You think it's Earth Patrol?" Derec said, then nodded. "A Spacer wouldn't shoot, either—"

"A Spacer would be calling us. Face it. Whoever this is, it's an enemy," Ariel said.

"We should have a good idea of our course and speed relative to Sol before he reaches near point," Derec said, nodding in agreement. "We can Jump any time after that now that you have the prob input."

The enemy spaceship wasn't going to ram, of course; its point of nearest approach was its "near point" with their course, but the two ships would be farther apart—it would then be ahead of them.

"And we won't provoke them," Ariel finished.

"What with?" Derec asked, feeling lightheaded.

"You know what I mean."

Then Derec had it: "We do have a weapon—"

"Comm!" she cried, at the breaking-crystal sound of the chime.

"I hope it's not a Spacer ship," she said, worried, as she opened the channel.

Both of them gasped at the face that appeared in trimensional projection above their board.

Oh no, Ariel thought. *Aranimas!*

The alien pirate's cold visage regarded them.

His face was vaguely human, but had definite overtones of lizard. The eyes, for instance, were widely set, almost on the sides of his face. They were barely close enough together to give him binocular vision—but, unnervingly, Aranimas didn't much bother with binocular vision. Most of the time one eye focused on whatever he was looking at while the other roved, apparently supplying peripheral vision.

At the moment he was focusing on Derec with both eyes. "Derrrrec," he said. High-pitched, trilling, his voice was the most hateful thing Ariel had ever heard. "Arrriel."

Glaring at them, he altered the focus of his comm and shrank to distance without moving, his humanoid figure coming into view from the waist up. In this view much of his alienness wasn't obvious, but they both had seen him in person. He was as tall seated as Derec was standing, and his disproportionately long arms had three times the span of a tall human's. Thin body, thin neck, domed, thinly haired head, pale skin. Dark eyes, angry now.

"Wherrre is the Key to Perihelion? You escaped with it instead of leading me to robots."

After a heart-stopping moment—Derec gulped, temporarily shocked out of his sickness—Ariel said, with only a faint tremor in her voice, "We lost it in the wreck. W-we've been in hospital on Earth—"

"You lie. I detected three bursts of Key static about this

143

planet. The firrrst, weeks ago, began elsewhere. The last two began and ended here. Only the Key broadcasts in this manner!"

They looked at each other sickly. Before they could speak, the pirate pulled a small, gleaming, gold pencil out of a pocket. Ariel choked, and she heard a gulp from Derec, too. A pain stimulator! It was, she knew, something like a human neuronic whip, but even more intense. Or perhaps Aranimas was just more violent with its use. It did no damage if not overused, like a neuronic whip, but no one was tough enough to take more than one "treatment" before deciding to cooperate.

"You will tell all, and tell trrrue, or I kill you slow with this."

They did not doubt his sincerity. Nor would he listen to anything until he had taken the ship apart. They couldn't just give him the Key, even if it could have been of use to him —it was initialized only for humans. He wanted robots, among other things—power most of all.

Derec reached over and cut the channel.

"We have another option," he said, turning to her. "We could use the Key, call agent Donovan, and put the whole problem in the laps of the TBI and whatever Spacer authorities are on Earth. Or we can try to deal with Aranimas ourselves."

"Deal with him—how?" she said skeptically.

"I don't mean bargain. Ariel, you should use the Key." His plans were clearly hardening as he spoke. "I think I can ram that clumsy ship when he closes with us."

Ariel felt herself pale. "No, Derec!"

"It's the only way! We can't let him live. He's too dangerous—"

"But—" Her face cleared. "We can use the Key at the last instant."

Derec looked at her. The burst of adrenaline that had washed away his illness was fading. She determined that she would not use the Key unless he did, and he seemed to realize that.

"Okay, that's what we'll do. We'll pretend to surrender—"

He reached for the comm, but she grabbed his wrist. "No, Derec, it won't work! He'll never leave this ship maneuverable while he closes!"

"It's the only chance we've got," he said. "Our only weapon is the jet—and the nose of the ship! I'd like to fire the rocket at him, but he'd never pass in front of it."

Ariel sighed, but she was unable to think of anything better.

"Okay. Go get the Key. I'll fly the ship."

Derec nodded in relief, clearly not up to it.

When they tuned back into the comm channel, Aranimas was howling in his nonhuman voice, so shrilly as to make her teeth ache.

"You will not brrreak communications again, humans! You—"

"Very well! We have conferred and agreed to accede to your demands," she said. "We ask only that you guarantee our lives, or we'll destroy the Key in front of your eyes."

"You will not destroy the Key! I kill slow—"

"Not if we're dead first," said Derec, sounding tired and exasperated—the sound of a father dealing with wrangling children. "We want your promise."

The alien fell silent and studied them for a cold-blooded moment. "Verry well. You have my promise I will not kill you if you give me the Key, undamaged."

Ariel had a moment in which she wondered if the alien might keep that promise. But it didn't matter; Derec was right. He had to die. She felt a momentary pang for the harmless and spiritless Narwe slaves with whom Aranimas manned his ship.

Derec pulled the Key out of his shirt and showed it to him. While Aranimas stared greedily at it, Ariel, at the controls, asked casually, "Shall we maneuver to match you?"

"No, I maneuver."

There was a tense few minutes while the alien turned from them to his controls, rolled his ship, waited, waited,

waited, then burned toward them. At the end of the burn the ship was not far away and still passing slowly. Again it rolled, now plainly visible: a vast, ungainly mass of half a dozen or more hulls stuck together. How Aranimas balanced that thing along a center of mass so he could fire rockets without spinning out of control, all without computer aid, Ariel couldn't imagine.

He's too close, she thought, panicky. They hadn't time to get much velocity for the impact—or to set the Key! Even as she thought, she glanced at Derec, who started squeezing the corners of the Key. She slammed the rocket on, spinning the ship on its secondaries—the gyro, more economical of fuel, was much too slow.

Aranimas might be flying a clumsy conglomerate, but he was a skilled pilot—and it was a battlewagon. It had adequate sensors even aft, where the rockets were. The pirate spotted their maneuver and blasted aside, not bothering to scream at them over the comm channel.

Ariel looked over at Derec, slammed into her seat by the acceleration; the Key was ready, but they weren't. The alien ship was above them, then beside them, even as she struggled to turn nose on toward it. Too late—Aranimas had slid aside.

Ariel instantly cut the jet and started to spin ship, not to get too far away—Aranimas's gunners would have them in their sights the instant they cleared the near zone. Aranimas shrewdly slapped on more side thrust when he saw which way she was turning, in order to widen the gap between them.

Then the collision alarm rang.

They heard Aranimas yelling for the first time since the battle began. Ariel fought them onto a line with the alien ship, too busy to look about.

"The rock is moving!" Derec cried.

The chunk of rock that had swung in behind them and had gradually been overtaking them was now accelerating toward them at about a Standard gravity—and the bolo registered the temperature of rocket exhaust.

Wolruf's face appeared beside the diminished figure of Aranimas on their board.

"Hold him, Derec! I come!"

What Aranimas said was not intelligible, but energy lanced from the big ship at the rock. The rock vaporized, its outline flashing away in puffs of incandescent vapor as the guns bore. Those same mighty weapons had vaporized cubic meters of ices and snow at near absolute zero on the ice asteroid where Aranimas had first found Derec.

Underneath the flimsy camouflage was a little Star Seeker like their own.

Ariel's vision dimmed as she cut in the rockets' full power. In a moment, she cut them off. Her head bobbed against the headrest, and the ship was again diving toward Aranimas. He rolled and blasted to avoid them, and something monstrous slapped their flank, making the ship ring.

"Puncture!" Derec gasped, but she had no time. She had to hold him till Wolruf got there—

Aranimas rolled his big ship again, and again blasted to avoid her, throwing off his gunners' aim. *Good job, he doesn't have computerized fire control,* Ariel thought.

She was confronted with a split-second tactical problem. In moments they'd be past the alien ship, too soon to roll nose-on toward it. Aranimas had seen their intent and was going the other way. So she rotated further in the direction the nose was pointed, to bring their tail toward the enemy.

At the critical moment she blasted, and fire splashed over Aranimas's ship. It must have rung like a bell. There was a great outrush of air and assorted particles. Ariel was grateful she couldn't see well enough to tell if the particles were kicking.

In a flashing moment they were past, and the reflected flame glare died, and Aranimas was moving again, fire spurting from points on the ungainly hulls. Another kind of fire flashed, their own ship gonged when hit, jolted again, as Ariel's head rattled against the headrest and alarms yelled; Derec was saying something as she spun the ship as rapidly as shaking hands would let her. *Mistake!* she thought.

Should never have blasted *away* from him; now they were far enough away for the gunners to sight them.

Clenching her teeth, Ariel rolled the ship again, trying to ignore the hits, hoping one wouldn't disable them—or kill them. A single stray bolt would—

"We're still in their near zone," said Derec, breathlessly. "Glancing hits only—"

True, she thought, smiling mirthlessly—*they were still alive!*

And then they had completed their roll, much farther from Aranimas than she liked, and she blasted back. No more hits; the uneven outline of the alien ship grew and grew in their vision screens, and she breathed more evenly.

Then she had a moment of wonder: she felt better because she was not going to be killed by Aranimas's gunners in the next few moments. But she was trying to commit suicide by ramming his ship!

Aranimas began to slide aside and she automatically corrected, centering on the dark bulk. What should she do?

"Wolruf is closing fast, but I don't know if she's still maneuverable," said Derec tensely. "She got hit hard."

"Give her a call?"

Then Aranimas's ship loomed monstrous and the alien had arranged a surprise: a gun on the hull swung to bear on them. What prodigies of effort had gotten it ready in the short time the battle had taken, they would never know. It was a full-sized gun, though its first bolt was weak, an aiming shot.

Aranimas's gunners were not the timid Narwe. They were starfish-shaped creatures about whom Ariel knew little; they avoided the light and breathed a slightly different atmosphere than the rest of the crew. She felt no compunction about them, and spun the ship aside. Aranimas saw that and moved to prevent her from pointing her rockets at the new gun.

A second bolt flashed at them, but the gunners lacked Aranimas's own savage efficiency.

"Another puncture, and our antenna's out," said Derec calmly.

His calmness calmed her, and she made one more attempt to ram. In turning away from her jet, Aranimas had run before their nose. She cracked on full power and they were hurled back into their seats. Her vision dimmed. She thought it was the power fading.

Too slow; the huge, bloated body of the enemy slid sideways even as it grew monstrous before them. Then the vision screen erupted in one pale flare, pale because the safety circuit wouldn't transmit the whole visual part of the flash: the sensor had taken the next hit from the gun.

"There went our bow!" Derec cried.

Ariel gulped, half expecting to see space before her, but they hadn't lost that much of the bow. With the vision out, she could only crouch, panting, at her board, the rocket off, hoping for—

"The Key—trigger it—" she cried, turning to him, knowing in a flashing moment that it was too late—they'd hit—

The ship jolted, and the impact was quite different from the gun hits. They were thrown forward against their straps, the ship shuddered, metal squealed, something broke—all in an instant—then they were free, the ship floating quietly.

Air hissed out, alarms still burring and shrilling. All communications out, no exterior view. Ariel touched her controls and the attitude jets responded; she could turn and burn again. But they were blind.

"Suits!" said Derec. "And see if the auto-circuit can give us more eyes."

Suits first, she thought. When the air goes out of a small ship, it can go fast. Should have had them on all along, if they'd had time.

They scrambled into their suits in a free-fall comedy that was deadly serious. Every moment Ariel expected the lancing fire of a hit, but the ship continued serenely on its way.

They didn't bother to try communications, knowing that

the gun's bolt, or the impact, must have destroyed the forward antennas. Vision, however, could be brought in from any quarter of the ship. Only the bow eyes were out. After a bit of fumbling, they found an undamaged sensor that bore toward their late battle.

"What . . . what is it?" Ariel asked, awed.

"I was about to ask you," Derec said. "You know more about Aranimas's ship, you were on it longer—"

"That was before my amnesia," she said.

"Oh."

"I think—one of the hulls, broken free?"

They had only a partial view of it—it was below the sensor's view. Only a spinning, irregular curve of dark metal, with an occasional highlight gleaming, here and there a projection—derricks, turrets, landing ports, sensors—and interior beams?

"It can't be the whole ship," Derec said finally. "But what happened to it?"

Ariel took a deep breath, found the air inside her suit rank with her sweat. "I'll turn around!" she said, chagrined. "I didn't realize how tense I was."

She wasn't thinking. *I'll never be a combat pilot,* she thought shakily. *Wasted minutes looking into a view I could've adjusted— Or do pilots get used to this kind of thing?*

But the human race had no combat pilots. No telling how well they could perform. Grimly, she thought, *if there are many of Aranimas's kind in space, we may have to learn.*

"Aranimas—he disintegrated!" Derec said.

The big composite ship was now a dozen big pieces in a cloud of hundreds of smaller ones. They looked at each other. Derec's face was as blank as she felt her own to be.

"Did we do *that?*" she asked.

"I don't see how—Wolruf!"

After a moment she nodded. "You must be right. But where did she get the guns?"

Derec just shook his head.

If anybody was alive over there, they weren't disposed to do any more shooting. The wreckage was retreating slowly. Ariel came to herself with a start.

"We've got to get back over there—"

"Frost, yes!"

"But how?"

It wasn't easy, but they worked it out. The view they had gave them bearings. They chose a spot that would enable them to miss any of the junk, and rotated the ship until its blind nose pointed along that bearing. Ariel then placed her hands on the board, looked into darkness, and thought, *now we find out how good a pilot you are, girl*.

In a moment she was back on Aurora, about to do her first solo takeoff. She had had that very thought, or something very close to it, and even more nervousness than now. Now, though, she was in shock. The memories went on and on, the takeoff, the acceleration seeming more fierce than ever now that she *had* to remain conscious, the relief as the jets shut down, and then the indescribable free, floating sensation of one's first solo orbit.

"Ariel?"

Her instructor—

"Ariel?"

With a shake, she brought herself out of it. "Sorry. Memory fugue." As her hands moved over the board—taking care to push the buttons on the real board instead of the remembered one—the memories went on, flashed back, picked up details. A whole chunk of her past restored to her by a chance thought, a chance repetition of forgotten circumstance.

She burned for ten seconds and rolled the ship to study the junk. There should be detectors back there that would tell them how fast they were moving relative to the junk, but they weren't working. The junk still seemed to be receding. Ariel rolled and blasted for another twenty seconds, again looked.

"That should do it."

They had only to wait, floating toward the wrecked ship aft-end first, ready to burn to brake down.

"How did she do it?"

"It's hopeless," said Derec.

Mandelbrot was trying to patch their hull.

"It's got to work," Ariel said, biting her lip behind her helmet. "Otherwise, Wolruf—"

The other Star Seeker had been hit harder than their own and was scarcely maneuverable. Mandelbrot, using rockets welded onto his body and a line gun, had brought them close together, with Ariel doing most of the maneuvering. There was very little air in either ship—and there was no spacesuit for the caninoid alien.

"We've been stressed too severely. The best we can do is temporary patching." Derec tried to rub his head, and his hand encountered his helmet for the fifteenth time. Frustrated, he let it drop.

"If it holds long enough to Jump out of here—" she said.

Derec shook his head. "Four Jumps to Robot City—five for safety," he said. "That's days of work checking courses and calculating. I wouldn't want my life to depend on that kind of patching. And we'll be maneuvering. That'll strain the patches even more."

"Something's got to be done! Maybe Aranimas's ship—"

Jumping at straws, and she knew it. "Even Wolruf doesn't really know how to fly it—assuming any of us had the arm reach for that control board. No computer aid, Ariel!"

She nodded soberly. "I know. It's not possible; it's these ships or nothing."

"Maybe there's air or food over there. We could use both."

They looked at each other somberly. It was not a pleasant position.

On a wrecked ship, barely maneuverable, with most of its instrumentation out, leaking like a proverbial sieve, on a trajectory that would take it somewhere near Procyon in a few million years, short on air, water, and food, with a friend on another, worse ship, sealed into a single room.

"Join the Space Service and see the stars," Derec said, forcing a grin.

Ariel grinned back, just as wanly.

The alien ship was all around them, and some of the pieces definitely had once been living. Derec, feeling none too good to start, avoided looking at them, though they were at such a distance that details were lost. His imagination supplied them. Many were Narwe, but there was a goodly number of the starfish-shaped dwellers-in-darkness he had glimpsed in his brief time aboard the ship.

"I'm amazed they aren't trying something," he said again. They'd both been saying that for nearly an hour.

"Derec . . . I think they're all gone."

It could be. But— "Dead?" he asked.

Many were. Ariel shook her head, though. "I don't think so. I think they must have Jumped out at the height of the battle."

Leaning forward, Derec eagerly scanned such of the surroundings as were visible, trying to count the hulls. It was no use. "I don't know how many hulls there were, and they all look different now. The central one, I suppose, had the hyperatomic motors. Maybe some of the other hulls did, too. I don't think there's more than one hull missing, though."

"You agree, then?" she asked, worried.

"I agree," he said. "Knowing Aranimas, if he were alive and here, he'd be shooting at us. With something."

"Yes." She was silent for a moment. "It's not likely that

all that damage could have been done by Mandelbrot."

Wolruf had dropped the robot off when she had braked sufficiently to bring the relative motion of the ships down to a level Mandelbrot's rockets could handle. The robot had made a landing on the alien ship, damaging one knee joint, and then had swarmed all over it, planting explosive charges at the joins of the hulls. The mighty ship had simply broken up.

"We already know that there were explosive charges at the hull connections," Derec said. Aranimas had dropped one of his hulls to make his escape at Rockliffe Station.

"Yes. He must have blown them all, got his central hull free, and Jumped."

"If he Jumped blind, he could be anywhere in the universe," Derec said. "Let's hope he never finds his way back!"

It wasn't something they could count on.

Half an hour later, Mandelbrot called them on the radio and suggested that they go lock-to-lock with Wolruf's ship. Presently, Ariel brought them together, Mandelbrot guiding them, and the open airlocks grated together. They were compatible, and with a little nudging clanked into position.

"This join will not hold air long," observed the robot. "We must charge it, and Wolruf must move fast, despite the bag."

They had been pumping their leaking air into bottles, to save at least some of it. Derec took one of the bottles to the lock, shoved its bayonet fitting into the lock's emergency valve, and opened the bottle. Presently Wolruf banged on the inner door, the outer door clanking shut behind her. Derec let the air continue to hiss to equalize pressure—but the bottle went empty first.

Muttering, he jerked it out of the emergency valve, which closed automatically, and turned to the manual spill valve. It took a good grip to hold that open, but after a moment pressure was equal and they hadn't lost much of their precious air.

Wolruf entered in a transparent plastic balloon, now half deflated under cabin pressure. She looked a little short of breath—or scared; Derec certainly couldn't blame her. It could not have been easy to flounder in free-fall, inside that balloon, through the other ship and the twinned locks.

The little caninoid emerged from the release zipper with a shake, saying, "Thank 'ou. It wass a nervous time. I 'ave grreat fearr of the Erani."

"We think Aranimas is gone," said Ariel.

"I 'ope so, but I do not understand."

Ariel explained tersely.

"He would sshoot, if he could," Wolruf agreed.

Mandelbrot's voice came over the radio. "I will enter the other ship and bring forth what items I can," he said. "You will need more organic feedstock for the food synthesizers, and of course air. Perhaps it would be wise to explore the alien ship also."

That was a thought. It made Derec more than a little nervous, and he could see that Ariel wasn't much happier.

"That wreckage is grinding around a good bit. Still, the bigger pieces are getting farther and farther away from each other," she said. "It should be safe—as things go."

"That apartment back on Earth looks more and more cozy every minute," said Derec with a weak laugh.

"I sstay behind and fly ship," said Wolruf. "I glad to do thiss; do not thank me!"

Laughing crazily, they floundered into their suits and crowded into the airlock with Wolruf's plastic bag. Normally it was used to convey perishable items across vacuum. Now they pumped it up to half cabin pressure, pushed it up against the inner door of the lock, and started the lock pumps. As soon as lock pressure fell below half cabin pressure, the bag began to push them against the outer door.

Their suits braced them against the push, and the expansion of the balloon speeded the removal of the air outside of the bag from the lock. When the outer door was opened they were shoved out—Ariel just quick enough to grab a handhold on the door, Derec grabbing her foot. Laughing again, they shoved the balloon back inside and slammed the lock.

Their first item was to transfer the undamaged antennas of Wolruf's ship to their own, and to replace the burnt-out or smashed eyes. The two ships floated near to each other, linked by the light, strong line. Derec had brought tools, and also made a stop-gap repair on Mandelbrot's knee. An hour of work saw that completed, while the pieces of the alien ship got farther and farther away.

They squeezed back inside the ship to rest, recharge their air, and eat. Ariel said tiredly, "How did you come to be here—near Earth—Wolruf?"

The caninoid snapped hungrily at synthetic cabbage. "When 'ou Jump with Key, I hear static hyperwave. I hear two burrsts static, and I get fix on one. I expect it to be Robot City, but iss not. We know coordinatess of Robot City. It a long way away, but Mandelbrrot and I Jump to follow. Dangerouss, one long Jump. But we darrre not make more, orr we lose bearings. Sso one Jump all we take."

She paused to gulp more food. They were used to her table manners.

"When we arrive at Earth, Mandelbrot make identification. He lissten to broadcasst—hyperwave still not worrking—and tell me, iss Earth, and explain Earth. We do not have to wonderr for long if thiss where 'ou went with Key. I hear two more burrstss static, close together, same place: Earth. I not know how 'ou use Key so close together."

"Simple," said Derec. He was tired and his head felt unduly light, even more than free-fall would explain. "The Key was focused on that apartment. Using it to leave anyplace else, even on the same planet, takes you back to the apartment. We won't starve—if necessary we can always go back to Number 21, Sub-Corridor 16, Corridor M, Sub-Section G, Section 5, of Webster Groves, in St. Louis City."

"Anyway, we wait. After a while, though, we detect hyperwave burrst of Aranimas's sship arriving, and we know therre will be trrouble. He also had detected Key use."

"How long has he known how to do that?" Ariel asked.

Wolruf shrugged. "Possible he always knew. Aranimass

not one for saying all he know. Or more likely he learrned since we left him at Rockliffe Station. Is obviouss when 'ou think about it."

"How so?" Ariel asked sharply.

"Obviouss, Key must be hyperatomic motor," said Wolruf, and Derec interrupted.

"I don't think so. The robots of Robot City learned to duplicate them—they may even have made the Key we have. I don't think humans or their robots could duplicate any such radical advance in science and technology as would be represented by the reduction of a hyperatomic motor to pocket size. I think the Keys are very compact hyperwave radios. These subetherics trigger the hyperatomic motors, which are elsewhere, and focused on the Keys."

"Ah, 'ou think motors are in Perihelion?"

Wolruf was a starship pilot too, and knew the theory of hyperatomics. "Probably," said Derec.

The caninoid made a sound of interest, paused to eat more, and resumed her tale after pondering Derec's conclusion. "Anyway, we sat therre waiting, and Aranimas sat therre waiting. We expected 'ou to use the Key and escape. Aranimas musst have been chewing nails and sspitting rivets. He could not know what wass going on, and Earth too big even for reckless one like him to attack."

"How did you know we were us?" Ariel asked, and Derec, head throbbing, tried to follow the logic of her sentence.

"When 'ou used 'our hyperwave radio, he musst have known. Aranimas burn to intercept, and we follow him. We fortunate to be closerr by half a solar orbit, get in firrst. Aranimas not sstop to think how lucky he be to have rrock to hide behind, going just his way almost as fasst as he. Only mistake he everr make."

Derec hoped it would be his last.

"What did you do to his ship, though?" Ariel asked, exasperated.

"Blow up. All time we waiting in orrbit, we were making

explosivess. Carbonite recipe in Dr. Avery ship data bank. I know enough chemistry to add oxidizer. Had to use food synthesizerr feedstock, but only one of me to feed, and I ssmall."

The robots had no doubt needed carbonite for the building of Robot City. Derec knew generally how it was made: it was a super form of black powder, using activated charcoal saturated with potassium nitrate or sodium nitrate. Since the carbon was nearly all burned up—it approached one hundred percent efficiency and was therefore nearly smokeless—carbonite was about ten times as powerful as TNT.

"Even so, it would not worrk if Aranimass had not panicked and Jumped. But he could not know what wass happening."

Derec nodded, immediately wished he hadn't; the room seemed to spin. "His panic is understandable," he said.

"Are 'ou all right?" Wolruff asked.

"No, but I'm not getting worse. I mean, I'm feeling no worse than before the battle."

Ariel broke in to explain about the chemfets, and Wolruf was concerned but unable to help. She knew nothing of robots, nor did any race she knew of, save humans.

"I hope 'ou will be well," she said, but clearly had her doubts. She seemed shaken by the idea of this invasion.

Derec thought of it as a disease, and at least had the hope that the chemfets were programmed with the Three Laws.

"Shall we go?" he asked. He turned and found Mandelbrot looking at him.

"What do you intend to do about this infestation?" the robot asked.

"Go to Robot City and either turn the problem over to the Human Medical Team or seize Dr. Avery and force him to reverse it—or both," said Ariel.

"I see. I can think of nothing better, for I do not believe that the medical and/or robotic resources of Aurora or the other Spacer worlds would be adequate to the task of eradication of chemfets," Mandelbrot said. "That then must remain purely as a final resort."

"Rright," said Wolruf. "We go find Dr. Avery. He worrse than Aranimass!"

The next step was to explore the alien ship. They cast off from Wolruf's Star Seeker and jetted lightly toward one of the larger, more intact hulls. They carried clubs, and Ariel a knife from the galley, but they found it airless and had little fear of survivors. There were none, as it turned out. Nor were there all that many bodies.

"Aranimass musst have sounded the recall and called them to the main hull," Wolruf said. "They would be valuable to him, of courrse."

Still, a good number of innocent Narwe—and not-so-innocent starfish folk—had died in the battle. They found nothing of immediate use in the first two hulls, and became depressed.

"We must have air, if nothing else," Mandelbrot said. "And we should also find organic feedstock for the synthesizers. It is, you tell me, five Jumps to Robot City. It will take at least three weeks, and then there is the final approach, and a reserve against emergencies. This hull will not hold air for three days. It can be patched up more, but probably not enough to hold air for more than a week. We will need four complements of air, and even so, I must spend every moment patching till the Jump."

"You'll be patching after every Jump," Derec said grimly.

Mandelbrot was right. They returned to the search, though the hulls were getting far apart now.

The next hull had been one occupied by the starfish folk, and they immediately gave up hope of finding air here; the strange aliens breathed a mix containing a sulfur compound that Wolruf called "yellow-gas." On the way out, though, they found a robot.

At Ariel's cry, Derec shook his head and took a deep breath. The robot, when he came into the open chamber where she was, seemed a breath of sanity in unreality: the shot-up spaceship, in free-fall and airless, was like an Escher print of an upside down world. The body of one of the starfish folk was stuck to one wall, a vicious-looking energy piston in one tentacled grip. Ariel and the robot were spinning slowly in the vacuum, drifting toward a bulkhead. She had leaped to seize it.

"It's dysfunctional," she said.

Timing his moves with hers, he intercepted them at the bulkhead and they turned their lights on it. It made no move, but whether it was speaking or not, they could not tell.

Mandelbrot entered while they were examining the robot's body. "Energy scoring on the head, and fuse marks here and there, mostly on the body. It looks like the starfish over there shot it up during the battle.

"How did it come to be in the ship?" Ariel asked.

"Hmm. I suppose Aranimas must have come upon it somewhere and captured it," said Derec.

"Where could he have found it?"

Derec considered. "Possibly it's one he found at the ice asteroid. But I doubt it. He was desperate for me to make him a robot. He'd have given me all the parts he had."

Mandelbrot fixed his cold eyes on the damaged robot. "This is a robot from Robot City."

"Yes." The design style was unmistakable to the trained eye.

"Let's get it into air; maybe it's trying to speak," said Ariel.

But back in the Star Seeker it lay as inert as before. Removing his spacesuit, Derec got out the toolkit and looked at Mandelbrot. The prospect of work on the robot made him feel better than he had in days. A matter of interest. They quickly learned that power to the brain was off. Reenergizing it, though, did no good.

"A near-miss from an energy beam might well cause brain burn-out without visibly damaging the brain," said Mandelbrot.

The positronic brain was a platinum-iridium sponge, with a high refractivity; it wouldn't melt easily. But the positronic paths through it were not so resistant.

"So we can learn nothing from questioning it," Derec

said, dejected. "Wait a minute. What's this?"

Clutched tightly in its fist was a shiny object. A shiny rectangular object.

"A Key to Perihelion," said Mandelbrot expressionlessly.

"Aranimas would have taken it away from the robot if he'd known it had one," said Ariel. "I wonder what the robot was doing with it?"

"We'll never know. Maybe it took the first moment it wasn't under observation to try use the Key. And the starfish caught it in the act." Derec gripped the Key and pulled it out of the fist. Instantly he knew it was different.

"It feels like two Keys built together!"

"It is," said Mandelbrot, peering at it. "One, I suppose, to take the robot from Robot City. One to return him to Robot City."

"Which is which?" Ariel asked.

Derec and Mandelbrot spent a few minutes determining that. They found that one Key had a cable plug in one end.

"I see," Ariel said, when they showed her. "A tiny cable, with five tiny prongs. It must be for reprogramming. I don't know what would plug into it—"

"Something like a calculator," said Derec, "to enable one to input the coordinates of the destination."

The other Key had no provision for changing its programming, and was therefore set permanently on Robot City.

"Not that it does us any good," said Ariel wistfully. "It's initialized for a robot. Too bad; we desperately need to get to Robot City, especially Derec. And only Mandelbrot can get there."

"That is true; Derec must go to Robot City soon, and the Key is better than three weeks in a ship, even if the ship did not leak," said Mandelbrot. "I will take you there, Derec." He wrapped his normal arm around Derec, half carrying him.

"What about us?" Ariel cried. "This ship is no safer for Wolruf and me."

Mandelbrot's mutable Avery-designed arm was already stretching into a long tentacle. "That is correct—it is very likely that you and Wolruf will die if you do not accompany us," he said. "Therefore, I shall have to take you all."

The tentacle coiled about Ariel and Wolruf and splayed out into a small hand at the end. "The Key, if you please, Derec."

Derec placed the doubled Key in the small hand. "At least Dr. Avery won't be expecting us," he said.

"He find out soon 'nough," said Wolruf.

Mandelbrot extruded another finger from the hand that held the Key to Perihelion. It rose up and pressed, in sequence, the corners of the Key, and waited for the activating button to appear. Knowing it was irrational, Derec felt the air get staler in the tiny pace of time it took. Then, Perihelion.

And then a planetary sky burst blue and brilliant above them. They were breathing deeply, standing atop the Compass Tower—the mighty pyramid that reared over Dr. Avery's Robot City.

DATA BANK

R. DAVID: This robot is a typical example of an Earthly robot. Like all robots, it possesses a positronic intelligence infused with the Three Laws of Robotics. R. David wears a blandly smiling face, a standard feature on all Earth robots, which are designed to reassure Terrans. The Terran economy is based on full employment, not full automation like the Spacer worlds. Thus robots are used only for those jobs that humans cannot or will not take.

Terrans rarely come into contact with robots, increasing their fear and dislike of them. R. David is cruder in appearance than the positronic denizens of Robot City because he has been designed to look less powerful, less invulnerable, and hence less threatening to suspicious humans. He lacks the streamlined and efficient appearance of the robots Dr. Avery created for Robot City.

ILLUSTRATIONS BY PAUL RIVOCHE

STAR SEEKER SHIP: Dr. Avery's small craft is the interstellar equivalent of an economy car, a small personal starcraft capable of transporting a maximum of six people. The Star Seeker model comes equipped with only the essentials needed to sustain life during an interstellar voyage. There are no luxuries. There is a food synthesis system, a water purification and recycling system, which includes a shower, and sanitary facilities.

The ship's communications system consists of hyperwave, microwave, and laser transmitters and receivers. The hyperwave antenna is mounted in a nacelle in the ship's nose, as far as possible from the hyperatomic engines to avoid disruption of the communications signal.

The ship's computer is a less-than-positronic intelligence, actually not much more than a glorified calculator and information storage system.

Like all interstellar ships, Star Seekers jump through hyper-

space, with massive thrusts of the hyperatomic motors that propel the ship at right angles to time and all three spatial dimensions simultaneously. Ships cannot jump without precise coordinates, so their guidance systems lock onto beacons in orbit around stars along the lanes of interstellar travel.

THE UNDERGROUND CITY OF ST. LOUIS: Terran cities are enclosed, largely underground, and entirely dependent on the Terran power grid. Light, ventilation, and climate control are all artificially maintained, and if power were to be disrupted for even an hour, it would mean the extinction of the city's population.

In the enclosed cities of Earth's future, citizens rarely travel beyond the city of their birth, and almost never go outside. Agoraphobia is so widespread as to be the norm of human behavior.

St. Louis, like the other enclosed Terran cities, is connected to the rest of the world by its communications systems, airport, and the highway system travelled mostly by robot-driven, or remote-controlled trucks.

Travel within the cities is accomplished on the expressways. There is some use of small trucks for transport of goods within the cities, but most freight is sent over a system of moving slidewalks. Personal vehicles are almost unknown, and are basically the prerogative of the very rich and powerful.

The city scene shown here is late at night. Normally, the streets and escalators are clogged with people.

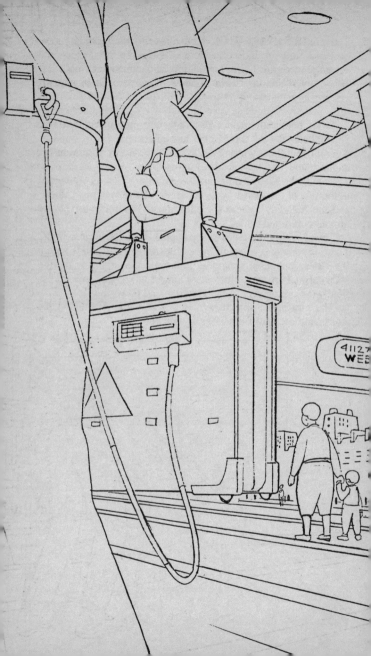

EXPRESSWAYS: This is the average citizen's primary means of transportation in Terran cities. The expressways move at varying speeds, with the slowest ones at the outside to make it easier to enter, and the fastest lanes in the center. There are expressways to all areas of the city.

To accommodate rush hour crowds, special rules go into effect, restricting access to certain lanes to the citizens with the highest ratings.

For Earthers, using the expressways is as natural as breathing, and Terran babies learn to use them as soon as they learn to walk.

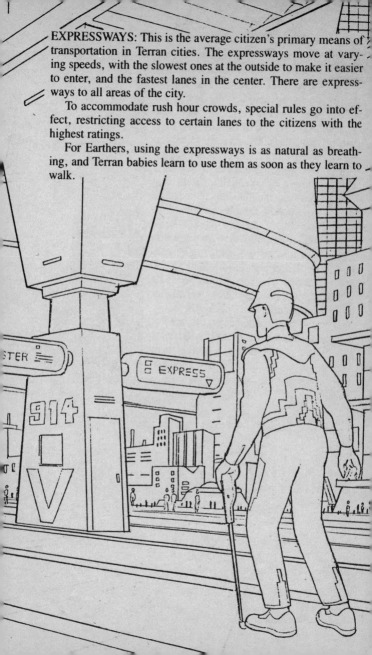

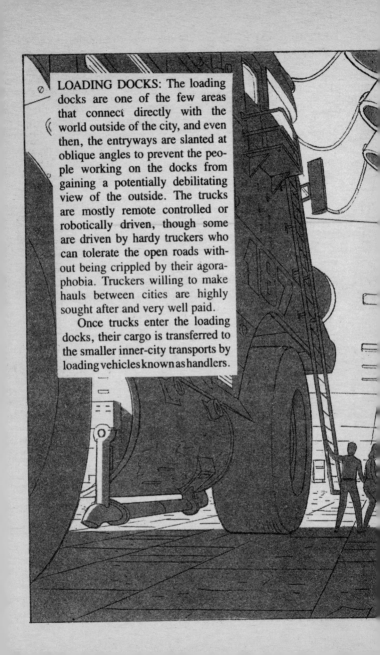

LOADING DOCKS: The loading docks are one of the few areas that connect directly with the world outside of the city, and even then, the entryways are slanted at oblique angles to prevent the people working on the docks from gaining a potentially debilitating view of the outside. The trucks are mostly remote controlled or robotically driven, though some are driven by hardy truckers who can tolerate the open roads without being crippled by their agoraphobia. Truckers willing to make hauls between cities are highly sought after and very well paid.

Once trucks enter the loading docks, their cargo is transferred to the smaller inner-city transports by loading vehicles known as handlers.

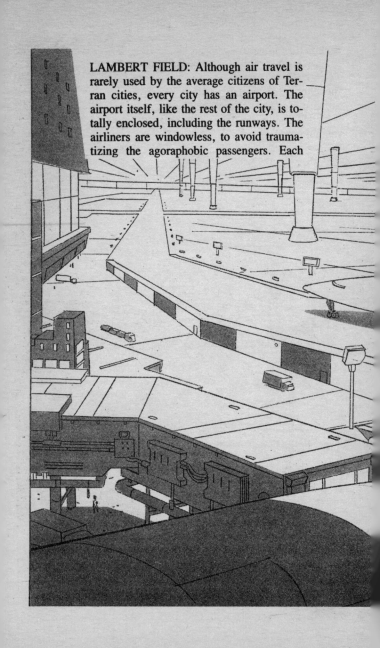

LAMBERT FIELD: Although air travel is rarely used by the average citizens of Terran cities, every city has an airport. The airport itself, like the rest of the city, is totally enclosed, including the runways. The airliners are windowless, to avoid traumatizing the agoraphobic passengers. Each seat on the airliner is equipped with a viewing screen that provides a constant feed of news and entertainment to occupy the thoughts of edgy air travellers. Sedatives are also provided for those passengers who wish to sleep during the entire trip, thus minimizing their trauma.

SPECIAL AGENT DONOVAN: Donovan is the agent in charge of the St. Louis office of the Terrestrial Bureau of Investigation. The TBI is the global investigative force, which is charged, among other tasks, with keeping tabs on all Earth-side Spacers in order to avoid any unpleasant incidents between the Spacers and the less-privileged Earthers.

TBI agents are a tough, well-trained corps of policemen. In common with his brother agents, Donovan is athletic, intelligent, and relentlessly efficient.

ROB CHILSON

A Kansas City area writer, Rob Chilson has lived in Missouri since the age of nine. He began writing at eleven, and was part of the last generation of authors to be trained by John Campbell. His first sf story was published in 1968. Among his novels are *The Curtain Falls, The Star-Crowned Kings,* and *The Shores of Kansas*. He is currently working on several series of stories in collaboration with such writers as Robin Bailey and William F. Wu. He is also doing another series, for *Analog,* about pocket brains.

Fantasy from Ace
fanciful and fantastic!